Praise for

Miles to Go

...a perfect blend of highly erotic sex and sweet romance...a unique and poignant romance... Fans are sure is to enjoy the latest addition to the Love in Xxchange series. ~ *BlackRaven's Reviews*

Miles to Go is a poignant, rough, romantic, sensual love story... ~ *Queer Magazine Online*

The story pacing is smooth...I found it entertaining and enjoyable... ~ *Literary Nymphs Reviews*

Total-E-Bound Publishing books by Bailey Bradford:

Southwestern Shifters

Rescued
Relentless
Reckless
Rendered

Southern Spirits

A Subtle Breeze
When the Dead Speak
All of the Voices
Wait Until Dawn
Aftermath
What Remains

Love in Xxchange

Rory's Last Chance
Miles to Go
Bend
What Matters Most
Ex's and O's
A Bit of Me

Love in Xxchange

MILES TO GO

BAILEY BRADFORD

Miles to Go
ISBN # 978-0-85715-746-1
©Copyright Bailey Bradford 2011
Cover Art by Posh Gosh ©Copyright 2011
Interior text design by Claire Siemaszkiewicz
Total-E-Bound Publishing

Published in 2011 by Total-E-Bound Publishing, Think Tank, Ruston Way,
Lincoln, LN6 7FL, United Kingdom.

MILES TO GO

Dedication

To the wonderful crew at the playroom,
who cheered on Max and Bo.

Prologue

Maybe one day he'd get used to seeing his boss and Rory looking so happy and mushy in love, but Max Jenkins kind of hoped he didn't. If any two people had ever been made for each other, it was Chance and Rory, and now with the addition of Annabelle to the household, both men almost glowed with joy. Well, Rory did, really, and it made the young man look even more angelic than he usually did.

It was something to see, especially for someone like Max, who'd never really seen what a happy, loving relationship could be like. His own parents had been…they'd just been a mess, was the nicest way Max could think to put it. Having grown up with that example, he'd pretty much decided he was meant to spend his life alone. Seeing Rory and Chance together, though, sometimes made him question that choice. Then he'd remember he had the blood of two insane, hate-filled, mean bastards running through his veins. That immediately killed off any hope he had of finding someone to grow old…older…with.

Not that forty-three was old, exactly, but damned if Max didn't feel ancient when he wasn't working and had too much time on his hands. Nights in the bunkhouse could just be hell, and often they made Max wish he was a drinking man, or prone to some other sort of self-medicating. Anything to shut off the thoughts and doubts and fears and loneliness that pressed down on him and threatened to smother him in the quiet hours before he could slip out the door and distract himself with work.

Max was confident in his work, and he knew his thick Southern accent could give some people the impression he wasn't too bright, or that he was laid back all of the time. Those people were the ones who weren't particularly bright, making judgments based on something as easily changed as an accent, and Max wasn't in any hurry to correct their thinking. In his opinion, if a person were ignorant enough to make such a snap judgement about him, that person wasn't worth the effort it'd take to set them straight.

Besides which, sometimes it suited him to be so easily categorised and dismissed. At least someone thought they had him figured out—Max was too confused about too many things when it came to himself. He wasn't sure he would ever puzzle them all out, or if he even wanted to. Sometimes it was just so much easier to float along in the comfortable confusion zone—it's what he knew, and if he could only be sure in his uncertainty about himself, well, that was still something.

Maybe even enough. Introspection—ha! Max bet a lot of people would fall over in shock if they found out he knew a big, fancy word like that—just wasn't his thing. That would involve examining his past, and he didn't really want to do that. Any time the past threatened to suck him down and swallow him whole, Max would find a way to occupy his mind.

Usually that involved a lot of reading, sometimes crossword puzzles. He tried that damned Sudoku and decided he'd rather just take a bullet to the head than wrangle numbers around. It pissed Max off to no end that he couldn't ever complete even one of those godawful puzzles, not without looking at the answers in the back, anyway, and what was the point of that?

"Crap, gonna be another one of those nights," Max muttered, tossing his hat on the couch. It bounced onto the floor, and he thought about picking it up then shrugged. It wasn't like anyone else lived here in the bunkhouse with him.

Later, he'd figure that was the exact thought that jinxed him.

Chapter One

Evenings in the bunkhouse should have been peaceful, but Max kind of hated them. Too much time alone since he was the only employee here at the Galloway Ranch. Well, technically Rory was the other hand, but since he and the boss had hooked up and got all moon-eyed over each other, Rory had packed up and moved into the big house.

Which left Max alone most evenings unless he was invited over for dinner with Rory, Chance, and Rory's sister Annabelle. Almost every evening one of those three checked in with him to see if he wanted to eat with them, but Max said no more often than not. Best to let family have time together — and maybe he felt a little like the odd one out.

Luckily everyone believed him when he'd tell them he was tired or wanted to watch some show on TV. Truth was, sleep was hard to come by, always had been, and as for watching TV, well, he tried but sometimes all those people laughing and loving on there just made Max feel more alone.

"Well, guess I'm in the mood for a big ol' pity party," Max muttered as he stepped into his bedroom. *Lord, I don't even want to be in my own company if I'm gonna be a whiny bastard.* Max snorted and started undressing, nearly landing on his butt as he tried to pull off his boot. Rolling his eyes at himself, he hobbled to the bed and plopped down on the edge. Bending over sent dull streaks of pain across his lower back, but he needed the boot jack. Once he found it, Max dragged it out from under the frame and shoved his boot heel in the u-shaped slot. That little piece of wood made getting his boots off so much easier.

After a quick shower, Max dried off and put on his boxers. Jeans and a ratty cotton shirt were next. He decided to forgo socks, which could be slippery on the wooden floors, and he didn't feel like putting his boots back on. It hadn't been too cold of a winter yet, just a few nippy days and some chilly nights. Max would have loved to have sat around in his boxers, but with Annabelle living on the ranch now, he never knew when it was safe to just let it all hang out. That girl tended to blow in like a blonde-headed tornado, not caring if Max might be stark-ass naked.

Not that he ever was, other than when he got cleaned up, but even then he wouldn't have put it past Annabelle to just throw open the bathroom door if she wanted to talk to him. Thinking about the possibility made Max's skin so hot he bet he fairly glowed, and not in a good way. He'd flat-out die of embarrassment if something like that happened; Max couldn't imagine someone seeing him in the buff. Even when Rory had lived here, Max had been careful to keep his stuff covered, and not because Rory was gay. Max didn't care about that. He was just...shy, which was probably stupid considering he was well over forty.

Max realised his mind was jumpy tonight, bouncing all over like a toddler who'd sucked down a bag of sugar and capped it off with a quart of caffeinated soft drink. He needed to settle down, and he needed to eat. His stomach was gnawing right through his backbone. He headed into the kitchen and opened the refrigerator, rubbing his rumbling stomach as he looked over his options for dinner.

Eggs seemed the easiest; if he was cooking for a full crew he'd have put more effort into it, but it was only him. Max reached in and grabbed the carton. He added a stick of butter, some shredded cheese that he'd have to examine closely before using, and a pathetic looking green pepper. He'd just set the food down on the counter by the stove and was fixing to go back and check the expiration date on the milk when the phone rang.

Figuring it was Rory or Annabelle, or maybe even Chance calling to nag at him to join them, Max muttered as he walked over to pick up the phone. Before he could even get a word out, a light tenor came through the line.

"Hey Max! How's it going?"

Max frowned and pulled the phone away from his ear an inch or so. Someone was awful perky. The man's voice sounded vaguely familiar, and like a smack to the head, it jostled his brain into gear. He kind of knew that voice.

"Bo?" Max knew it had to be the blond haired man he'd met up at the big house a while back. *Bo Daughtry, Chance's former fuck buddy.*

"Who else? You expecting someone—another man, maybe, to be calling you?"

"Uh." *Well that sounds smart.* Max tried to make sense of the questions but they just weren't registering. He'd only met the man the one time, and yeah, they'd got on, playing cards in the bunkhouse when things had heated up between Chance and Rory at their place. To be truthful, Bo had made an impression on Max—he just wasn't sure *what* kind of impression that was.

A soft snicker came through the line. Max's right eyebrow started twitching as he wondered if Bo was laughing at him.

"Max? You there?"

Max debated hanging up in mid-answer—he remembered someone saying a long time ago if you wanted off the phone with someone and couldn't figure out how to do it nicely just to hang up while you were talking. Supposed to seem like an accident that way since most people wouldn't cut themselves off. But he wasn't sure he wanted to get off the phone just yet. At least Bo was someone to talk to.

"Yeah, just..." Max turned, his gaze darting around the room before settling on the makings for dinner. "Just about to start cooking, s'all. Got a little distracted."

"Oh, hey, you haven't started yet, have you?"

Max thought Bo sounded almost wistful, which didn't help Max feel any less confused. The twitch sped up. "N-not yet, no, why?" What was Bo up to? Did he want to get together again or something? And what would Max say if he did? Last time, he'd been awful friendly, touching Max's arm a lot and smiling almost constantly. Max guessed Bo was just one of those happy, touchy-feely types.

Bo huffed then cleared his throat. "Well, I'm about to pass through on the way to San Antonio. I thought maybe we could grab a bite, if you wanted."

It was on the tip of Max's tongue to say no, but the eggs didn't look as appealing as they had a few minutes ago.

And he was in one of those broody moods, the kind where he'd sit and stare at the TV or the wall and try to keep from thinking too much. Maybe getting out for a bit was just the thing he needed. Maybe.

"You don't want to stop in and see Chance and Rory?" Max asked, still reluctant though he wasn't sure why. "Rory's sister Annabelle is here now, too." Not that she'd appeal to Bo. Rory had met Bo for the first time when Bo had been trying his best to get into Chance's britches. Apparently they'd had something going years ago, and Bo had shown up thinking to hook up with him again. Or something. From what Rory had said, Max didn't think Bo had been looking for anything permanent.

"Ahhhh…" Bo drew the word out then gave another of those huffing sounds. "As nice as I'm sure it'd be to meet her, I kind of didn't feel like hanging out and watching Rory and Chance get all sweet and cuddly with each other. Green is not a good colour on me."

Max crinkled his nose, trying to make that stupid twitch stop. He finally pressed at it with his fingertips. "What do you mean, green ain't your colour?" Max knew jack shit about stuff like what colours looked best with what skin tones and such. It dawned on him what Bo meant just as the man started explaining.

"I mean, I got a bit envious, seeing those two together—not that I want either one of them," Bo rushed out. "I just…well, I guess what I mean is, I want what they have. With someone else, of course."

Surely that sensation of something tickling down his spine was just some weird coincidence. Or maybe he'd pushed that damned twitch down through his shoulders. Max lifted his fingertips. *Nope, still there.*

"So, anyways, you up to meeting me in town? We could meet at Cowboy's. I heard they have a great chicken fried steak."

Max's stomach rumbled loud enough he wouldn't have been surprised if Bo heard it through the phone. Obviously one part of him was all for eating out. Max looked at the packaged cheese. He was pretty sure there was a funky grey-green tinge to it.

"Yeah, okay. What time?" The twitch ramped up a few tics then stopped as Bo's laughter filtered into Max's ear.

"Soon as you can get here, cowboy. I'll get us a table."

"That sure of me, were you?" Max mumbled, but he was talking to a dial tone. He shrugged and hung up the phone. Why wouldn't Bo be sure of him? It wasn't like Max had anything else going on in his life, and he remembered telling Bo almost that exact thing when they'd been hanging out before.

* * * *

Cowboy's wasn't too crowded on a Monday night, and Max was grateful for that. The place was fairly popular with the locals, so sometimes it was packed. Max wasn't sure he could have handled that tonight. He wasn't surprised he was nervous; he'd never been one to get out much, preferring the company of horses and cattle to most people. At least with the animals, he didn't have to worry about making a fool of himself, or being laughed at. Max knew he was odd, different from most folks. He didn't need anyone getting a kick out of it, though.

You're being ridiculous. Ain't like you got a sign on your head saying you're weird as hell. Max lifted his cowboy hat and wiped at his forehead, brushing off the sweat caused by nerves before settling the brim just so. Then he got out of his truck and pocketed the keys. He slammed the door shut with more force than he'd meant to, and it drove home how unsettled he was. Why, though, was a mystery to him. Surely he wasn't so set in his routine that he couldn't alter it now and again without getting rattled.

Max took a couple of deep breaths and envisioned a layer of calmness coating him. In his mind's eye, it was a feather-soft pinkish cloud encapsulating him. It was always pink, he reckoned because he'd read somewhere it was a soothing colour. Wrapped in his imaginary pink cloud, Max walked across the parking lot and pulled open the door to Cowboy's. The interior of the place was over the top country, with horse shoes and old tack hanging on the walls. Along with that there was more rooster and chicken prints and figurines than should ever be in one place. But no one came here for the décor.

There was a panicked moment where he worried he had forgotten Bo's face, but then the smiling blond man was right there in front of him, walking with a slight bounce in his step. Bo was slightly shorter than Max, who wasn't anywhere near tall himself, but the blond had a presence big enough for a giant. He just exuded personality, and his mega-watt smile had more than one person in the place craning their necks to keep Bo in sight. If Max could have only picked one word to describe Bo, it'd have been glossy. The man seemed to shine all over, from the tip of his blond head to the toes of his red boots. Even his lips looked slick. And why was he noticing that? Max didn't have the chance to consider it any longer because Bo parted those lips and words tumbled out.

"Max! Glad you made it!" Bo thrust out his hand and Max was shaking it before he knew what was what. The fissure of electricity that skipped up his forearm startled him for a second before he put it down to Bo's vibrant nature. Maybe it was like passing on a super power or something, and Max would wake up and find himself as happy as he acted like he was, or as happy as Bo was right now.

Right. And I'll be six foot tall and solid muscle to boot. Idiot. Max shut down the internal dialogue and returned Bo's grin, although probably not as brightly. He didn't have that inner glow.

"Bo. Good to see you." Was it his imagination or did Bo's fingers brush over his palm when they separated hands?

"Got us a booth," Bo said, doing something with his eyes that made Max think the guy had a couple of eyelashes floating around in them. "I hope that's okay?"

Max grunted an assent then followed Bo over to the booth. His gaze drifted over Bo's lean form as Max wondered what it was that made Bo so...so...*Bo*.

"Didn't know if you'd want tea or beer so I didn't order you a drink." Bo slid into the booth and looked up at Max. There was something in his hazel eyes, a question or doubt, Max wasn't sure but it didn't look right in those big eyes. "You drank some of both when we played cards and, well, I didn't know how long it'd take you to get here."

The smile on Bo's faced dimmed slightly as Max remained silent. He wasn't trying to be an ass, he was simply attempting to work out what was going on with Bo. Which was a waste of time, because he'd only met the man once and didn't know him, not really.

"Actually," Bo frowned and flicked a glance at the table before looking back at Max while he slid into his seat. Bo folded his hands together on top of the faded red tablecloth. Max noticed the white tint to the man's knuckles. Was Bo nervous? "I wasn't certain you'd show up."

The fluttering in his stomach had to be due to lack of food, Max decided. And as for the way his heart pinched, well of course he felt bad for worrying Bo. Max didn't like to hurt people, not that he thought he had the power to hurt Bo, but still. He tried his easy smile and was relieved when Bo answered with a rather tremulous grin. At least it was better than a frown.

Max plucked off his cowboy hat and set it beside him. He ran a hand through his hair, smoothing it back as he politely set Bo straight. "'Course I came. I wouldn't have said I'd be here then not show up." Actually, it kind of irritated him that Bo would think so little of him. They'd spent hours talking and playing cards—*but that doesn't mean Bo knows me any more than I know him.* "Besides, you said chicken fried steak. Those are magic words to a hungry cowboy."

Bo's lips tipped up more, setting off dimples in his cheeks Max didn't recall seeing before. "Ah, got it. If I want to spend some time with a friend who happens to be a cowboy, all I have to do is mention chicken fried steak. Shame I didn't learn that sooner."

The waitress appeared before Max could think of a witty reply, which was good because his brain seemed to have shut off as soon as he saw those dimples. Why, he hadn't a clue, but he felt warmer, too. Maybe the restaurant had the heat running, although he didn't think that was necessary considering he hadn't even needed a jacket this evening. He glanced up and spotted a vent but didn't feel any heated air coming from it. Probably it was on a timer or something then, though he couldn't recall feeling a warm draught at all. He'd just sort of heated up from the inside out, but that didn't make any sense. It must have had something to do with being middle-aged.

They placed their orders, waving away the menus beforehand. Max fiddled with his napkin as he waited for his glass of sweet tea to be brought out. His throat was unaccountably dry considering he didn't feel thirsty.

Bo propped his elbows on the table, his eyes widening when it wobbled under his weight. He jiggled it as if making sure the table would hold then shrugged. "So, Max, have you had any wild and exciting adventures since the last time I saw you?"

Max nearly snorted at that, which would have made a hell of a mess considering he'd just started to take a big gulp of his tea. Obviously Bo didn't know him at all if he thought Max ever did anything that could be described as wild or adventurous.

Max swallowed his drink, his eyes watering when he tried not to cough as an ice cube slid right on down his throat with the sweet liquid. It was no use, and he slapped a hand to his mouth as he hacked and spluttered. Bo's eyes lit up, the laughter starting there before it spilled from his lips.

"Sorry."

He didn't sound sorry to Max. Max's cheeks burned as one of his worst fears came true. Bo's laughter drew the attention of the other diners, and Max wanted to melt right into the vinyl bench. Shit like this was why he didn't want to go out much in public. He hated being the cause for other people's amusement. Max had learned at an early age that being mocked and snickered at hurt like hundreds of tiny barbed hooks burying into his heart.

His hand trembled as he carefully set the glass down. Spilling his tea would just add more fuel to the fire of his personal hell. The best he could hope for now was a dignified exit. Max reached for his hat even as he started scooting towards the edge of the booth, keeping his gaze averted from Bo. He muttered something about needed to go home, or at least he hoped that's what he said. In truth, his heart was pounding so fast he could hear it clear up to his head, making him deaf to everything but the sound of his impending panic ringing in his ears. He absolutely refused to look across the table.

Which was why he didn't see Bo move until the man was right there, blocking his exit, making it impossible for Max to stand. Max's jaw dropped open when he looked up at Bo, then nearly hit the floor when the blond started to sit. Max didn't have any choice but to slide back over to the far side of the bench, pressing his shoulder against the wall there, or he'd have himself a lap full of Bo. He managed to plop his hat on the table and cringed inwardly. His momma would have walloped his ass for that.

Max fingered the brim for a minute, trying to smother his embarrassment. His cheeks were so hot they stung, but he forced himself to cock his head and look at Bo out of the corner of his eye. "I should go." Before he did anything else that got him laughed at.

Bo shook his head. He leaned over, his shoulder brushing Max's, and lifted the hat off the table. A slight snap of his wrist sent the Stetson over the table and onto the seat Bo had been occupying seconds before. Bo sat back and crossed his arms over his chest.

Defensive body language. Max had read that in one of those crime books he'd bought at the grocery store. *But what does Bo have to be defensive about? Maybe that was a load of horse shit. Maybe it doesn't mean anything except he wanted to cross his arms.* But when Max turned his head further to see Bo better, there was that same doubtful expression on the blond's face, along with what Max thought was guilt. Bo's next words confirmed it.

"I'm sorry, Max. I didn't mean to make you feel like you had to leave. I-I didn't know it'd upset you if I laughed." Bo nibbled his lower lip for a second, leaving the flesh a deeper rose colour when he released it. "I honestly thought you'd laugh, too. I'm sorry."

Some of the tightness in Max's chest eased even as he acknowledged to himself that a normal person wouldn't have got all butt hurt over something so stupid. It was just more proof that he was a total mess when it came to being like everyone else.

Bo nudged him and looked increasingly worried. "You know, that whole 'laugh and the world laughs with you' thing? I wasn't laughing *at* you, I was laughing *with* you. Come on," Bo pleaded softly in a voice that seemed to feather over Max's skin. "Help me out here, Max. I didn't mean to screw up. I-I was hoping we could be friends. I guess after that night we played cards and got on so well, I thought, maybe…"

Well now I feel like a complete jerk. Max finally unstuck his tongue from the roof of his dry mouth long enough to lick at his equally dry lips. He was kind of afraid to try drinking his tea again. His voice scraped past parched tissue and sounded squeakier than he would have liked, but at least he finally got the words out.

"It's fine. I just…" Max lifted his head a little and peered around the room, unable to keep looking into Bo's intense eyes. "I get nervous, don't feel comfortable around many people." Max gave in and picked up the glass, slick with moisture. He concentrated on not dropping it while he took another sip, this time barely parting his lips to keep from choking on another ice cube.

It almost didn't matter. He could feel Bo watching him. Max cut the man a glance as he swallowed and nearly spluttered all over again when Bo licked his lips. Unless

Max was wrong, Bo was watching his throat as Max drank. He forced the sweet liquid down and kept his eyes on Bo in what he hoped was a discreet manner. Max took another swallow. Bo's gaze seemed to follow the liquid's path right down Max's throat, which was weird, and a little unsettling. *Maybe Bo's just really thirsty, too.*

If Max's hand shook a bit when he set his glass back down, he figured it was from nerves. He was still concerned about doing something foolish. It had nothing to do with the way Bo's cheeks had pinked or the strange light in his eyes that made it look like Bo glowed from the inside out.

Thirsty, Max thought, and he reached across the table for Bo's sweaty glass of tea. Instead of picking it up, Max slid it over until it bumped Bo's fingertips. Bo blinked and shook his head then turned away to grab his drink.

"Thanks," Bo murmured.

Max nodded. The man obviously needed to whet his whistle. "It's good tea, not too sweet." And could he get more pathetic, talking about tea instead of something a little more interesting? Max racked his brain and finally found something not so asinine to talk about. "So, what have you been up to? You on your way home?"

What tension had remained in Max slowly bled out as he sat back and listened to Bo talk. The man sure could chatter, which Max was glad of since it saved him from having to try to do much talking.

After they finished their dinner and were waiting for the waitress to bring them their slices of pecan pie, Bo leant back and rubbed his stomach. He'd moved back across the table shortly before their chicken fried steaks had arrived, and now Max found himself watching for the reappearance of Bo's hand as he made slow circles over his belly.

What with the table in the way, Max could only catch sight of part of that hand, and it didn't occur to him until he started to lean over a bit, to question why he was so fascinated by what Bo was doing. What was wrong with him? Max pressed his shoulders against the back of the seat. Bo would think he was some kind of weirdo if he kept it up. And he really needed to tune in to what Bo was saying, something about going to a club —

"…but if you can take a couple of days off, you could drive to San Antonio and we can hang out. I'll take you down to the River Walk, every tourist has to go there. There's this great chocolate store there, they have the best toffee and these caramel apples that are bigger than my fist." Bo held up one clenched hand and waved it around. The man looked so happy and hopeful, but Max shook his head.

"I can't, Bo. We got a couple mares ready to deliver any time now, I'm sorry." Max was, but he was also relieved to have a legitimate excuse for saying no. As foreman at the Galloway Ranch, it was his responsibility to make sure the births went smoothly, and even though the vet was on call if she was needed, Max just didn't want to risk not being there when those foals were born. Seeing those little babies stand up on their wobbly legs was one of the best things Max ever got to experience. And yeah, it got him out of having to leave his comfort zone, but that really was secondary in this case.

Bo seemed to lose some of that sparkle even as he nodded and dropped his hand back to the table. "Yeah, I understand. Maybe another time then." He didn't look like he was holding out much hope for it though, and Max just wasn't up to offering him any. Luckily the waitress arrived with their pie then and the subject was dropped as the two men enjoyed their dessert.

Later that night, as Max laid in bed, he kept puzzling over the way Bo had seemed so disappointed when Max had said he couldn't go to San Antonio. That bothered him almost as much as the way he'd been so fascinated with Bo rubbing his stomach. Max huffed and rolled onto his back. Behind his closed lids, Max kept seeing that hand caressing Bo's shirt, pressing lightly to rub against the muscles underneath.

Without really thinking about it, he brought his hand up and mimicked the movement. He guessed it felt okay, but probably not the same as if he'd been doing it to Bo, or if it'd been Bo's hand touching him — Max's eyes snapped open at the shocking thought. It wasn't the idea of a man touching him that shocked him, Max's reaction would have been the same if Bo was a woman — which kind of didn't make sense, but the fact was, he'd never really thought about anyone touching him like that, not for a long, long time. And he didn't quite know what to make of it now that he had.

* * * *

Max was in the barn the next morning when he heard the arguing. Already exhausted from another sleepless night, he tried to ignore the squabbling, because siblings argued, didn't they? But Rory and Annabelle weren't getting any quieter, their voices rising and anger edging each word they spewed at each other. It made Max's stomach roil and his chest tighten, and his fight or flight instincts were trying their best to take over.

A particularly loud shout from Annabelle made Max's head spin with memories, and his hands tightened on the pitchfork until his grip caused pain to shoot up his forearms. He wanted to run and hide, and therefore, he wouldn't, though he just might go snap some sense into those two kids.

Setting the pitchfork down carefully, Max took a deep breath and forced himself to relax, pushing away the unpleasant memories that seemed more determined lately to rise to the surface. He pasted a smile on his face and stepped out of the barn, intending to put an end to the bickering. A big hand clamping down on his shoulder nearly made him squeak, and Max glanced behind him to find Chance shaking his head at him.

"They'll work it out," Chance murmured, nodding at Rory and Annabelle.

Max looked at the two siblings, who were flapping their hands in the air as if to emphasise that their opinion was the right one. "The hell they going on about?"

Chance squeezed his shoulder then patted it before removing his hand. "Well…"

Something about the man's hesitation had Max slowly turning to face him. "Well, what?"

Chance glanced at the scene the two younger people were putting on, grimacing when Annabelle's loud refusal to cave in to her brother's demands punctuated the air. "It seems that Annabelle doesn't feel right about staying in the house any longer — with us."

That would explain the comment — the loud comment — that Max had heard moments ago. Annabelle had proclaimed that she was perfectly capable of making her own decisions about where to stay, and Max had wondered what the hell she was talking about. Now he knew, sort of. Then he wondered why.

"She got a problem with you and Rory?" Max glanced at Annabelle, trying to envision that. She'd seemed more than happy about her brother's choice of a partner when she'd arrived, and the same at the few dinners Max had attended up at the big house.

"Nah, nothing like that," Chance assured him. "She just thinks that if she's going to be working here, she should be treated like any other employee when it comes to her living quarters. Any other employee being you, of course."

Max thought it might be more than that, like maybe Annabelle didn't want to impose on her brother and Chance's privacy, but he wasn't going to butt in here. Then it dawned on him where she'd be staying.

"You're gonna put a woman in the bunkhouse with me?" Max burst out before thinking. The unwanted image of Gloria Steinem driving a spike through his balls flashed through his head and he cringed. "I don't mean it bad, just..." He couldn't figure out a good way to finish that sentence, so he shut up.

Chance snickered and slapped him on the back. "I know what you mean, it isn't something that you've ever had happen to you, but neither is working for a gay man and his partner, is it? I'd think a woman in the bunkhouse would be easier to accept..." Chance paused and gave him a considering look. "Or maybe you're worried about something happening there?"

Max could feel the blush burning his cheeks, but he looked Chance straight in the eyes. "No, sir, I wouldn't dare mess with Rory's sister. I like my job."

"Well, then." Chance grinned, and Max felt more than a little trepidation shoot down his spine. "Looks like you're getting a bunkhouse-mate." With that and a wink, he walked over to Rory and pulled his lover aside, effectively shutting down Rory's rant.

Annabelle glanced his way and Max nodded, letting his usual grin slip into place. She bounced down the porch steps and jogged towards Max.

"I'm sorry about the pissing contest," Annabelle said as soon as she was close enough to be heard easily. "I wouldn't have thought my brother would be so old-fashioned."

"I'm sure he was just worried about you," Max replied, then wondered exactly what it was Rory had objected to. The idea of his sister living with Max? Or was it just that he wanted better for Annabelle than a bunkhouse?

"Do *you* have a problem with it?" Annabelle's eyes were as dark a blue as her brother's, and she held Max in place with the power of her midnight gaze.

Max wanted to be diplomatic, and not make Rory or Annabelle mad. He didn't really have a problem with a woman sharing the bunkhouse with him — it wasn't like he found Annabelle attractive, though she was cute and everything. It'd just surprised him, but as Chance had said, it was actually easy to accept. "It ain't up to me, but if you decide that the bunkhouse is where you want to stay, I don't have a problem with it."

"Good, because I'd rather you be comfortable than not," Annabelle replied. Max took that to mean she would have stayed in the bunkhouse even if he had spoken out against it.

But I didn't, and who knows, maybe it would be nice to have someone else around. Although what we'll talk about other than work is beyond me. Come to think of it, it might not be any different than before. Max wasn't sure whether that was a good thing or a bad thing, because sometimes, if he was honest with himself, he almost ached to have someone to be close to.

Annabelle living there wouldn't change that at all. She was a nice young lady and all, but there wasn't any spark, and Max wasn't hoping for one anyway. There would probably be some polite conversation, and Annabelle would almost surely want to eat dinner with Rory and Chance most nights, so Max would be alone. As he glanced back at Rory and Chance huddled together on the porch, their arms tangled around each other and both of them looking so…*happy*, Max tried to tell himself that being alone was what he'd always wanted, or at least what was best for him.

The problem was he couldn't seem to believe it quite so firmly anymore. He acknowledged the truth of that thought—and damned if he didn't blame it for what happened a few days later.

Chapter Two

Max was in the North field doing one of his least favourite tasks — repairing the fence. They'd had a storm blow through the night before that had been more wind than rain — a lot more wind. He was guessing that might have something to do with the tree he'd found on the smashed fence. The result was that Max had got to play with the chainsaw first before tackling the repair job.

Using the chainsaw was almost worth having to fix the fence. There was just something fun about it, and the concentration it took to keep from cutting off his limbs kept his mind from wandering in directions he'd rather it not go. Lately his mind seemed determined to think of Bo at odd times — Max snorted. *Right. Odd being most of the time.* He'd given up freaking out about it and put it down to having a real — he hoped — friend for the first time in a very long time. Sure, Rory, Chance and Annabelle were kind of friends, but Chance was his boss, and Rory was too, and Annabelle was related to Rory. It wasn't quite the same thing, and even though he hadn't seen Bo since they'd ate dinner together at Cowboy's, they had talked on the phone a couple of times, and it had been...nice.

"And I'm just wasting time," Max muttered. He got the chainsaw started and forced his attention on keeping his parts attached like he preferred them. All too soon he had the tree cut into pieces he could load into the truck bed by himself. He might not be the tallest, buffest looking guy around, but he had a surprising strength. It didn't take long for him to load up the soon-to-be firewood. Now he only had the fence left to deal with, and he tried to get himself motivated.

"Quicker I get started, the sooner I'm done with this." That didn't really help one damn bit. Max knew he'd never make it as a motivational speaker, and besides, someone had taken his personal motto and made it into a shoe slogan — *Just Do It!*

He wasn't doing 'it' or anything else as he stood there holding the ground down. Max sighed and wondered what was wrong with him — he never hesitated to work, not even when it was something he *despised* doing. There were things he disliked more than stringing barbed wire, but he couldn't think of a single one right then.

Max reached for the roll of wire he'd brought with him. His walkie talkie snapped with static, then Annabelle's voice came through loud — really loud — and clear.

"Hey, Max, you busy?"

Max could hear the smirk in her voice. He slid his two-way off its clip and thumbed the button. "Nah, Miz Annabelle, you just caught me right before my nap." Max never would have thought he'd tease Rory's sister like that, but after an initial bit of awkwardness on his part, they'd got along great since Annabelle had moved into the bunkhouse. Max had never had a little sister of his own —

he was the next youngest in a brood of eight brothers — but he'd always wished he did.

"Well, Rory was going to come out and help you, but he and Chance went tearing out of here after they got a phone call, so that leaves me to help you with the fence. I'm on my way."

Max started to ask what was going on, but Annabelle would be here soon enough, and he had work to do in the meanwhile. He wasn't the type of man who'd sit around and wait for help to arrive.

Max had just started to reset the first post when Annabelle pulled up to the gate. She'd driven rather than ride her horse up, a sign of her hurry to get there. Max swiped at the sweat trying to run into his eyes as he greeted her.

"You got here pretty fast," Max said as Annabelle opened the gate. She had thick leather gloves tucked into her waistband and a brown paper sack in one hand and a couple of thermoses tucked under the other arm.

"Yeah, well, I didn't want to be slacking, you know, and I brought some sandwiches and tea." Annabelle waved the bag. "You've been out here for hours, you have to be starving."

He was, and damn near boiling in his clothes in the Texas. The humidity after even a little rain could make a cool day miserable to work in. His long-sleeved denim shirt and undershirt were both damp in spots. The promise of cold sweet tea had him jerking his gloves off and tucking them away. "Appreciate it, Annabelle."

"You're welcome," she replied, handing him a thermos. Annabelle flicked him a worried look. "So Chance got a phone call, like I said, and he and Rory left almost as soon as the phone hit the cradle. They both looked pretty upset."

Max uncapped the thermos and took several refreshing swallows of the cool, sweet liquid. Nothing tasted so good as chilled sweet tea when he was thirsty. He thumbed the excess off his lips and tipped his chin at Annabelle.

"They didn't say who called or where they were going?" That wasn't like either man—normally if something came up, they called Max on the two-way and told him about it. The fact that they hadn't could only mean that whatever had happened was bad enough to have rattled them something fierce.

"Nooooo, not exactly." Annabelle looked at him, just a darting glance as her cheeks pinked. "I kind of looked at the caller ID because…because they just don't act like that, right?"

Max nodded, trying to be patient. He had a nervous itch creeping over his spine—that *never* signalled anything good.

"It was from a St. Joseph's hospital, with a 210 area code. That's San Antonio, isn't it?"

Sweat dripped into his eyes as he scrunched his eyebrows. *Damn, that burns!* "Yeah it is, but who—" Max's stomach plummeted. There was only one person both men knew well enough to worry about. The same man who had caused Max more than a little internal turmoil. Annabelle's next words had that turmoil increasing exponentially, and his knees turning to jelly.

Annabelle's voice was soft as she said, "All I heard Chance tell Rory was that Bo was in pretty bad shape." She looked at him curiously. "Who's Bo?"

Max's heart kicked hard in his chest as Annabelle's question chilled him more than the tea ever could have. He felt cold clean through to his bones, and had to tense every muscle in his body to stop the shudder that tried to tear through him. "He's a friend," Max murmured, his voice oddly calm compared to the chaotic emotions trying to burst past the rigid control he always bound them with. He wasn't prone to hysterics and wasn't going to start being so now. "A good friend."

"How good?"

Something in Annabelle's voice set off a tingle of alarm in Max as he looked at her. Her eyes were narrowed and he thought if ever anyone could peer into someone else's thoughts, it'd have been Annabelle with that intense blue gaze. One of her blonde eyebrows arched and it dawned on Max what she was really asking.

"Not that kind of friend." How he kept from snapping it out was beyond him. Between being embarrassed at her even asking and his worry for Bo, Max was only tenuously keeping his temper in check. "He's someone Chance used to know...like that," he explained. "I met him a while back when he showed up here thinking to, you know, *visit* with Chance."

Annabelle snorted and rolled her eyes. "And Rory didn't kill him?" Then she frowned and glared at him as if Max had done something offensive. "Then why did they go rushing out of the house like he was, well, not like he was some horn dog who came sniffing around for a fuck."

The tip of Max's ears burned as anger made his temples throb. He had to remind himself that Annabelle didn't know Bo, and even so, she wasn't entirely wrong about what he'd tried to do. *But still!* "You haven't met him. He ain't like that now, least not with Chance and Rory — or me," he added before she could ask.

"Huh." Annabelle didn't look particularly mollified though she wasn't glaring, exactly. "So he's just everybody's friend." The way she said it sounded kind of snarky, but Max wasn't going to call her on it.

"Yeah." Max turned and strode to the truck he'd just loaded then opened the driver's door. He'd left his cell phone charging since the battery was messed up and it tended to go dead minutes after unplugging it. He leaned in to make sure he didn't stretch the cord too far. The missed call icon caught his attention, but he ignored it in favour of dialling Rory's number. The first call rang a few times then went to voice mail so Max hung up and tried again. Rory answered on the second ring and started talking before Max could so much as grunt.

"Max, I've been trying to call you. Did you get the message? Bo's hurt. He's at St. Joseph's in San Antonio, and we don't know what happened except he wasn't the one who called us, some nurse did and she said Bo managed to give them Chance's name. Took them a while but the nurse finally found a number and he's been beat up. We don't know how or why or who did it, but as soon as we do…" Rory finally trailed off.

It was stupid to feel hurt that Bo had given Chance's name instead of his, but Max couldn't stop it or the twinge of jealousy hearing that caused. Then he processed the rest of what Rory had said and a cold ball of fury coiled in his stomach.

Someone had hurt Bo, deliberately from the sound of it. Max tried not to let any possible scenarios for what happened develop in his mind. He didn't want to think about Bo maybe having done something that got him beaten, like coming on to another man's guy. He didn't want to assign the blame to Bo at all, and he wouldn't, because even if Bo *had* put the moves on someone he shouldn't have, that didn't mean he deserved to wind up in the hospital over it. Guilt slammed into Max as he recalled one of the conversations the other night in the diner—Bo asking him to visit. It had been, in Max's opinion, a spur of the minute invitation. Bo had mentioned going to a club first. If Max had gone to San Antonio, would Bo not have been lying injured in a damned hospital now?

"Let me know as soon as you find anything out," Max muttered as he closed his eyes. The guilt was almost as strong as his anger at whoever had hurt Bo, although maybe he should just put both emotions squarely on himself. It wouldn't have hurt him to take a couple of days off. The others would have been able to handle it if the mares had foaled, which they hadn't. That had only been an excuse anyway. Max just hadn't wanted to deal with a situation that would have been uncomfortable for him.

"What'd you find out?"

Max set the phone down and shrugged. "Just that Bo got beat up somehow. Rory said they'd call with more information when they got it."

The hand on his shoulder startled him, and he turned around partially to dislodge it and partially because he was confused about why Annabelle had touched him. The sympathetic look on her face made him feel even worse than he already did, though, so he started to walk past her only to stop when she caught his wrist. Max looked at her hand on him first then up into her eyes. He hoped she wasn't this touchy-feely all the time. She sure hadn't been up to now.

"I'm sorry about your friend getting hurt," Annabelle said in a voice so soft he had to strain to hear it. "I hope he's okay, and I'm sorry if I was judgmental about him coming on to Chance. It obviously didn't make Rory hate Bo, and even though my brother can be naïve at times, I don't think he'd go rushing off like this for someone who wasn't a decent person."

Max grunted at that then pulled away and headed back to the downed fence. If Annabelle hadn't insisted they eat first, he wouldn't have bothered, but he let her have her way and managed to eat his sandwich even though he didn't really taste it. Annabelle was blessedly quiet as they ate, not trying to strike up a conversation. Max was grateful. His thoughts were filled with 'what-ifs' and 'should have dones'.

Those were bad enough, but even worse was owning up to why he'd refused Bo's invitation. The fact was, Max was scared to say yes. Bo made him feel things he just didn't know how to deal with, and even now he wouldn't examine those things too closely. Max had been alone for more years than not. He hadn't felt any particular desire to be with another person, not in any way. He knew that made him well past odd and it wasn't something he cared to shout out from a rooftop or anything. There were reasons for it, he imagined, but he'd never delved too deep in his psyche to search them out. It had just been easier to accept it and keep to himself outside of working relationships.

And yet, here at the Galloway Ranch, he'd kind of made friends, of sorts. Work friends, at least. It'd been impossible to keep Chance and Rory neatly labelled as just bosses, and there was Annabelle. Max hadn't been around a lot of women; he'd pretty much stayed on whatever ranch he'd worked on except when he couldn't get out of it. Even then, it hadn't been like there'd been women throwing themselves at his feet.

Max snorted softly. Like he'd have noticed if any had. On the rare occasions when he was out somewhere where there were female folk, he ignored them. Max kept his mind on what needed to be done, and he hardly saw anything or anyone not related to that task. Probably God himself could walk right past Max and he wouldn't notice.

Well, I'm going to hell for that thought if nothing else. Guess even Daddy's belt couldn't whip the sacrilegious thoughts out of me. And I sure don't want to go thinking about all that shit right now. Most of his memories regarding his parents and home life were as painful as thinking about Bo hurt, scared and alone.

Max closed his eyes as he chewed the last bite of his sandwich and pictured Bo, his eyes twinkling, something hot and mysterious in their hazel depths, his broad smile and those deep dimples. The Texas sun must have poured on more heat despite it being winter, because Max felt it roll over him like a wave. The muscles in his stomach quivered and the insides of his thighs shook as fantasy Bo laughed, the light tinkling sound shooting from Max's memories into his bones, making him ache in a way he couldn't fathom.

"You about ready to get back to work now?"

Max nodded as he opened his eyes, almost resenting Annabelle for chasing off that phantom Bo. Annabelle stood and dusted her hands on her jeans and tipped her head towards his truck. "I didn't hear it ring, but do you want me to go check anyway?"

"I'll do it," Max said as he stood. His knees popped and his lower back cramped a bit. He grimaced as he shot Annabelle a bashful look. "It's hell getting older."

"Beats the alternative, which is *not* getting older," Annabelle pointed out. "And all the plastic surgery and crap like that in the world doesn't stop someone from getting older. It just makes them look really fucking creepy for the most part. So the way I see it, getting older beats being dead, you know?"

He couldn't really argue with that. Max checked the phone and didn't see any missed calls or texts. It occurred to him he might not hear it if it went off while he was working on the fence. "You got your cell phone on you?" he asked as he peered over his shoulder at Annabelle. She nodded. "It okay with you if I text Rory and Chance and tell them to call your number if they hear anything?"

"Of course, like you even have to ask." Annabelle plucked her phone out of her shirt pocket. "I'll text them."

With the matter settled, Max tried to get some of his focus back on work. He wouldn't be doing anyone any favours if he got careless with the barbed wire. Despite his best attempts, though, Bo remained in his thoughts, his laughing visage almost constantly on Max's mind.

* * * *

It took every bit of Max's willpower to finish the fence and the rest of his work without stopping to call either of his bosses. The need to know what was going on with Bo was pressing down on him. Max told himself it was because Bo was a friend of his—it had nothing to do with the dreams he'd had about the lithe blond man that left him shaken and confused when he woke up.

Those dreams, along with the fantasies Max's brain seemed determined to create, always sent his body into a state of arousal and his mind spinning with confusion. He'd never been particularly attracted to anyone, which might seem strange for someone his age, but Max just accepted it as a fact. Having been raised in a violent fundamentalist household, sex was something that was discouraged—except his folks apparently hadn't got the memo since there'd been eight kids.

Any normal inquisitiveness a child might have had wasn't allowed in his house, and since Max had plenty of older brothers to learn from, he'd buried every trace of sexuality as deeply inside himself as possible. More than one of his brothers had been brought before the family for masturbating. His father always made the guilty boy strip then proceeded to beat him sometimes to unconsciousness with his thick leather belt while the rest of the family was forced to watch.

Well, not forced, not all of them, Max admitted to himself. His ma had always ordered the number of strokes, and his oldest brother had frequently cheered and jeered. Sometimes Max thought it was a miracle he was still alive and as sane as he was. And he couldn't go there, hadn't ever really been able to and probably never would.

* * * *

Max stirred the pot of chilli on the stove. The cornbread was done, nice and golden with just that hint of a sweet taste he loved. Hopefully Annabelle would, too.

"Sup's on," Max called out, hoping she'd hear him now the shower had stopped.

"Be there in a sec," came her faint reply. The bathroom door opened minutes later as Max was filling the two bowls with the fragrant chilli. "Oooh, corn bread, too! Tell me it's the sweet kind…"

Max chuckled despite the tension that had been eating away at him for hours now. "Yep, it is. Got you a chunk right there at the table."

"Oh, yum!" Annabelle took her bowl and grabbed a spoon from the silverware drawer, thanking him as she did. She pulled out her chair and plopped down. "I haven't heard from Rory yet."

Max stirred the chilli in his bowl, wondering if he could even keep it down. *What the hell is wrong with me?* The swirls in the orange-red stuff seemed particularly fascinating. "Him or Chance'll call as soon as they're able. They ain't thoughtless jackasses." Which meant that whatever happened to Bo, it must be really, really bad to have kept them from calling.

Or maybe it meant it wasn't serious, and that's why they didn't feel the need to call and let him know if Bo was okay—it was confusing and frustrating and Max felt a rare surge of temper. He excused himself, ignoring Annabelle's concerned expression, and put his food away.

Stepping into the bathroom, he shut the door and leaned against the sink. He'd felt such a sudden burst of anger that it left him shaking, his fingers trembling even as he tried to grip the cabinet. The urge to throw his bowl, smash it against the wall and do the same with anything else he could break, had come and gone in a flash, but *damn,* it had scared him. There were too many memories of his pa's violent temper that Max carried around with him—he wouldn't add his own.

He wouldn't be his pa, not once, not ever. He'd put a bullet through his brain before he ever hurt people like his pa had. Same went for his ma and most of his older brothers—he would *never* be the hate-filled monsters they were.

"I ain't him, I ain't any of 'em!" Max forced himself to look in the mirror. He tried to find any signs of the cruel people who'd raised him. Not in his features—he looked how he looked and that was all there was to that. No, what he was looking for was in the eyes, that spark in the depths there that was just...*off,* intense in a way that was terrifying and full of the promise of pain and punishment.

Max could see nothing like that in his eyes, but that was little relief. He'd felt that surge of anger—what if he'd been able to see his eyes then? What if—

A tap on the bathroom door startled him so badly that his hand slipped and he barely missed slamming his face into the mirror. "Hey, Max, you okay in there?"

Max's sense of humour tried to kick in, but he kept it quite a bit cleaner than he would have if Annabelle had been a man. If that made him sexist, well, he was sorry, but he couldn't bring himself to be crude around any woman.

"Showerin' ain't the only thing to do in here, you know," Max pointed out. If it'd been Rory or Chance, he'd just have yelled that he was taking a shit and leave him alone. He just could not do that with Annabelle, though he suspected it would embarrass him a lot more than it would her if he did.

"Well, duh, but I didn't hear any—"

"Jesus, Annabelle!" Max choked out. "What are you doing, sitting out there listening? Go away and leave me to take care of my business!" Though at this point, he thought he may never be able to do his business again, not with Annabelle in the bunkhouse.

"Relax, I'm just teasing you!" She thumped the door for emphasis. "I pick on Rory and Chance the same way—all three of you are easy prey, so worried about offending *the girl*."

Max didn't have an answer for that. "Annabelle..." His cell phone vibrated at his hip, saving him from digging himself into a deeper hole. From the other side of the door he heard Annabelle's phone chime as well. Surely it was Rory and Chance calling. Max snatched the phone up, a glance at the screen confirming the call was from Chance.

He tapped the button to take the call as he brought the phone to his ear, his palm slippery with sweat.

"Chance, what's going on?" Max glanced at his reflection. He looked pale and stricken and he couldn't stand to see himself, so he studied the sink instead.

Chance sounded exhausted and disgusted when he replied. "Rory told you we got a call from a nurse at St. Joseph's earlier. She told us that Bo had been brought in yesterday, unconscious and damn near beat to death."

Max felt like an elephant sat on his chest. He couldn't breathe, couldn't speak, and something inside him was threatening to burst.

"He didn't have any ID on him, nothing, he was...he..." Chance's voice hitched and Max gripped the phone tighter as he began trembling. He clamped his teeth to keep them from chattering or biting his damn tongue in half. "Someone beat him and dumped him out in a field on the southern outskirt of San Antonio. It's...he's...fuck!"

While he'd known Bo had been beaten, hearing even those additional details made it so much worse. It hit him like a physical pain, ripping him open. Max's legs gave out and he landed hard on his ass, the wood floor ensuring that a solid *thunk* would be heard throughout the bunk house. "Is he..." Max swallowed and forced the words out. "Are you telling me he didn't make it?"

"No!" Chance nearly shouted. "Oh God, Max, that isn't what I meant! He's...he's in bad shape—I mean, he looks like shit, but he'll be fine. Someone delivered a fierce beating on him, and he looks like...like death warmed over, but he isn't going to die."

Max closed his eyes and leant back against the toilet, trying to get himself under control. His eyes burned and the tip of his nose tingled, but he managed to keep it together, except for the shaky breathing and the tremors that still shook his body. "That's...that's good then."

"Yeah, it is," Chance agreed. "Anyway, when Bo woke up today, he managed to give them his name, and mine for the emergency contact. Rory and I kind of freaked when we got that call. I'm sorry you didn't hear from us again sooner. We wanted to wait until we knew something, and frankly the staff here has been reluctant to tell us much of anything. If Rory hadn't managed to charm one of the nurses, we might still be waiting for information."

"No, it's fine," Max assured him. "Is Bo's family coming up there?"

"He doesn't have any family," Chance said. "None that will claim him. Bo doesn't really have anyone."

"Not having family ain't always a bad thing," Max said, shocking himself with that slip of personal opinion. He tried not to let anyone ever see anything more than his laid-back persona and the hard work he did. Still, it was already done. "You're bringing him here, ain't you?"

Chance was silent for a solid minute during which Max tried not to beg. "He's being released in a couple of days, and he's going to need some friends, and some help, too. Rory and I already went to his place and packed up as much as we could fit in Bo's SUV and our truck. Is it okay with you if we bring him home?"

Max nearly rolled his eyes. "Chance, you're the boss, you can bring home whoever you want to."

"That doesn't mean I have to be an ass, though. I just wanted to check, I thought you and Bo got along fine, but..."

But WHAT? Max wanted to shout it. He wished Chance would just say whatever it was he wanted to say and be done with it already so Max could shower and collapse into bed. His body ached like a bitch and he'd been through the emotional wringer twice today, at least. "But what?" He finally asked when Chance didn't seem inclined to continue.

"I guess…" Chance sighed, the sound whooshing into Max's ear with the force of a small tornado. "You seem all right with me and Rory. I guess I just wanted to make sure you wouldn't have a problem sharing the bunkhouse with a gay man if Bo decides to stay once he's healed. We're going to try to talk him into it, if you and Annabelle are okay with that."

Oh God! Max's dick hardened so fast he felt light-headed. Having Bo here would be hell, but not for any reason other than the fact Max felt things for the man he just hadn't felt for anyone.

"Max?" Chance's voice sounded a little louder, a little harder. "Is that going to be a problem?"

"No, you know I ain't one of those bigots," Max snapped, then cringed when he realised what he'd done, but damn it, Chance should know him better. "And I ain't one of those dumbasses who thinks every gay man is out to take my ass, either, so you can quit painting me with that homophobic brush!" Fuck, he was going to get fired if he didn't get his mouth under control!

"You're right," Chance surprised him by saying. "You've never done or said anything to make me think you're like that, and I apologise."

Max liked the fact Chance didn't make any excuses, no 'I apologise, it's just been a shit day and the stress got to me, blah blah blah'. A straight-out apology had always meant more to Max than one followed by excuses.

"Apology accepted, and I'm sorry for snapping and talking to you—"

Chance cut him off with a sharp, "Don't even." Max heard Chance exhale and waited, felling sure there was more to be said. There was, but not on the subject of Max mouthing off.

"Can you and Annabelle handle things there if Rory and I stay in San Antonio? We'd like for Bo to have someone here at least."

Max wanted to be there himself, but he couldn't say that without Chance asking him questions he didn't really want to answer. "Yeah, we got everything under control." He told Chance about the tree and repairing the fence and assured him once again everything was fine before they finally ended the call. Afterwards, Max sat on the side of the bathtub and rubbed his temples. He was so confused. These feelings for Bo were just so alien to him. If he were normal like everyone else, he wouldn't be experiencing what he suspected was his first crush at the ripe old age of forty-three.

For all of his adult life, he'd kept people away, afraid to let anyone to close lest they find out what a mess he was. And he had feared for years he'd turn out like his parents and siblings. Even though he hadn't so far, and he didn't truly believe he ever would, sometimes the doubts would creep in, especially when he got angry.

Max groaned and rubbed his temples so hard he got light-headed. He wished he could scrub all those memories away. What he wouldn't give to be able to go back in time —

"Idiot." *Stupid to even think like that.* He'd learned a long time ago that imagining a happy childhood only made the reality of his abusive one hurt worse. A sound in the hall alerted him just before there was another knock on the door.

"Just a minute," he called out as he stood up. "Almost done." Annabelle grumbled something he couldn't quite hear clearly as he walked over to the sink. He turned the water on and cupped his hands under it. A couple of splashes and he finally dared to look in the mirror. Other than dripping wet, he looked the same as always. Max tried smiling, relieved when it didn't appear strained. As long as he could keep that smile in place, Annabelle shouldn't be able to tell his insides were churning almost as much as his mind was.

* * * *

As Max laid in bed staring at the ceiling an hour later, he tried to imagine what it was going to be like having Bo around, possibly even *right here* in the bunkhouse. His dick had been hard since firming up in the bathroom earlier, and Max was beginning to ache with the need to come. It infuriated him that he still felt too inhibited to masturbate most of the time. Twenty-six years he'd been gone from his parents' house, and his head was *still* fucked up.

Groaning, Max ignored the throbbing erection tenting his boxers and rolled onto his stomach. The wrinkled sheets felt good against his aching shaft, and if he rubbed a little as he drifted off to sleep, well, that was his body taking over, wasn't it? It wouldn't be the first time he'd woke up stuck to the sheets.

Chapter Three

Max and Annabelle both were waiting on the porch of the bunkhouse two days later when Chance pulled up into the drive. Rory parked behind him, having driven Bo's SUV. Max let Annabelle rush down the steps in front of him, not wanting to appear in a hurry to see Bo. He just hoped the need he felt to do so didn't show in his expression.

"He's asleep in the back seat," Chance said as he got out of the truck and gently shut the door. "I almost hate to wake him, he hasn't been sleeping much. The doctor said he had nightmares most of the night—"

"They know who did this?" Max asked, tamping down the anger beginning to boil in his stomach. As much experience as he'd had with that emotion the past few days, he figured he should be able to control it better.

"No," Rory said as he walked over. "Police have no clues who the guy is who did this. "

"Well, they have Bo's description of the asshole," Chance corrected. "At least that's something for them to go on."

"What does he look like?" Annabelle asked before Max could, which was okay with him because somehow he'd moved over to the passenger door—and when had he grabbed the door handle? Max peered in the window. He sucked in a breath at all the bruises on Bo—and that was just the ones he could see on his face and arms. Bo was too still and that glow Max always saw around Bo, that he always imagined when he thought of the man, wasn't anywhere in sight. It was wrong, more wrong than just about anything Max could think of. He listened to Chance's answer while he wondered if Bo would ever recover the aura-like essence that had both fascinated and intimidated Max.

"Big, about six-three Bo guessed. Plain features, blond," Chance said. "And a real sick bastard to pick on someone Bo's size and kick his ass like that."

Max glared at Chance. "That in there? Ain't no ass-kicking, that's a beating some chicken-shit motherfucker delivered likely without giving Bo a chance to fight back." *Fired, I am so fired.* Max felt a hand on his shoulder and turned his head to find Annabelle smiling at him, her eyes shining. *Shit, I cussed and cussed in front of a woman!* Sure, he'd slipped up before and he really did try not to treat Annabelle any different from the men he worked with, but this time just seemed worse, and his upbringing came slamming back into him. Max opened his mouth to apologise.

"Don't you fucking dare," Annabelle snapped. "And if my brother and his love toy give you any shit about it, I will handle them. Maybe permanently." She winked and patted his shoulder before stepping aside so he could open the door.

"Holy—" *Shit*, Max finished silently, because Bo had looked bad through the tinted window, but without that dark shield? Both eyes were swollen, bags and dark blue and purple bruises surrounding them. Some kind of bandage was strapped over Bo's nose, setting it or holding it on for all Max knew. The right cheek had a long gash closed with several stitches, and there was another right by his earlobe. His lips were split, the top sporting a few stitches, the bottom painfully huge with a deep cut in the centre. Even Bo's chin was bruised, and another strip of stitches ran in a diagonal across his chin.

All of it fed Max's fury, but what really made him want to kill whoever did this with his bare hands, was the bruises and stitched gash on Bo's throat. Bo had been choked by his attacker, from the front obviously, as Max could clearly make out the blue-black thumbprints left behind on Bo's skin. The guy must have really been trying to kill Bo; the bruises were so deep, and there was another set right above the first that Max had noticed. Those swollen eyes moved slightly and he realised Bo wasn't asleep after all. How much of the conversation had Bo heard?

"Come on." Max gently reached for Bo's hand, intending to take it and tug slightly. The bruises and gashes—defence wounds? He wondered—stopped him flat. Max glanced back at Annabelle's gasp and shot her a look that he hoped said 'Cut that out'. She nodded and Max looked at Chance.

"Where *ain't* he hurt?"

"Ah…" Chance looked chastised rather than angry, so Max had hope he hadn't got himself fired with his little tantrum. He really needed to get his easy-going persona firmly tacked into place.

A grunt from the truck drew Max's attention back to Bo. He leaned in and offered his hand to the injured man, unsure if he was awake or not after all. His eyes could have just been moving around while he dreamt—and maybe Bo hadn't heard any of that conversation then. Max hoped Bo hadn't heard it, he didn't need to think about the sick fuck who had beaten him and tossed him out in a field like a bag of trash, especially not right now.

Max squinted as he tried to figure out whether the injured man was awake or not. Bo's eyes were so swollen, Max wasn't certain he'd know if Bo was peering at him or not, although he thought he saw a sliver of hazel under there. "You awake, buddy?"

Bo grabbed Max's wrist, his grip surprisingly strong. He half-pulled half-pushed himself up as Max held his arm steady, allowing Bo to dictate how much to exert himself. God, just watching Bo move made *Max* hurt. Chances were, Bo wasn't just beat in the face and arms, his body had probably—

Max's blood chilled in his veins. Chance had said Bo had been dumped in a field—nude. Did that mean…? Max wasn't going to ask. He couldn't bear to think of someone hurting Bo, especially not like that. But surely Chance would have mentioned—or maybe not. Max knew enough about male pride and egos to think being raped was something most men wouldn't want to talk about, much less admit to.

Bo grunted and tugged, and Max forced away thoughts that were guaranteed to drive him insane. "I take it you mean move, huh?"

At the slight nod from Bo, Max stepped back, slowly helping Bo from the truck. His arm slid around Bo's waist as the injured man's feet touched the ground. Max told himself the reason it felt so good to hold Bo like this was from relief that his friend was alive, even if he was battered all to hell.

The problem with telling himself that was, he couldn't make himself believe it. Not when Bo fit so perfectly against his side. Not when the touch of Bo's hands brought such peace and joy to Max's heart that he felt almost whole for the first time in his life. Not when parts of his body were starting to rise inappropriately—and not when all he wanted to do was take this man home and wrap him in the softest fabrics and keep him safe from all the evil shit in this world.

The only thing Max could believe was that he...was...so screwed.

* * * *

Bo felt like shit. Just about every part of him hurt, and all he really wanted was to lie down and sleep until he was healed. Maybe forever, even, since he wasn't sure he'd ever be completely well again, at least not in his head. The physical injuries would be gone in no time compared to that; the mental recovery seemed insurmountable. He didn't know if he'd ever feel safe or happy again.

Rory, Annabelle and Chance were huddled together whispering and gesturing. After a minute of concentrating on hearing what they were discussing so intently, he thought he knew what they were trying to figure out— where to put him up. The issue seemed to be whether he'd be better off on the couch or in the guest room. Frankly, Bo didn't care just then. He wanted to lay down somewhere and go back to sleep, or pretend to, at least. The nightmares made actually sleeping kind of difficult. He started to turn away and crawl back into the truck since nothing had been settled yet. Standing up was just too exhausting at this point.

"Stop before you hurt yourself worse," Max whispered when Bo started to pull away. "We're all being a bunch of dumbasses, ain't we? Should have had this figured out before you got here. "

Bo looked into Max's warm brown eyes and could have wept at the compassion and regret he found there. Sure, Rory and Chance had been kind, had come when he needed them and been better friends than Bo had a right to expect, but they hadn't looked at him with such tenderness, only pity, which made Bo want to curl up and die. It almost made Bo wish he'd had the nurse call Max instead, but as awful as Bo looked now, he'd looked even worse then, and he might have been beat to hell but he still had his pride. The idea of the man he was sort of infatuated with seeing him lying bloody and damn near broken in that hospital bed had been too much. Although, what with the kind look in in Max's eyes, and not a hint of revulsion at Bo's appearance anywhere to be seen in his expression, maybe he should have just had the nurse call Max instead. It'd have been comforting in a way having Chance and Rory there hadn't been even though Bo was grateful they came.

"Where do you wanna sleep?" Max asked. Something in his tone made Bo think it wasn't the first time Max had asked.

Bo wondered what Max would say to 'with you', but since he couldn't speak without it feeling like his throat was being ripped to shreds, he settled for tipping his head towards the bunkhouse. It was a little further away than Chance's house, but Bo had just realised something. He didn't feel nearly as scared standing there with Max. And after all, Max was the only one who'd thought about him, really thought about him just now. The other three were still in there little huddle. There was also the fact that Bo didn't want to intrude on Chance and Rory any more than he already was.

Max looked past him. "Y'all okay with Bo making his own decision?"

The other two men inclined their heads, and while they didn't look happy, they didn't object when Max led Bo to the bunkhouse. The woman — Annabelle, he assumed — started walking towards him and Max.

"We should probably put Bo in the middle bedroom, the one with the pair of twin beds," Annabelle said as she stepped up to Bo's other side. "We could take turns sleeping in there, or I can do it." She paused as they helped him up the steps. "Or maybe Bo would be more comfortable if you stayed with him."

Bo felt Max tense beside him. Was it fear, or something else that made him do that? Bo glanced at the man and saw the blush that had darkened his cheeks. Max didn't look angry, or scared. Maybe it was the pain meds that Bo had taken, but he thought Max would look just like he did now if he were a little turned on. Of course, he'd probably never get to know what Max in the midst of arousal looked like. The man hadn't responded to any of Bo's flirting, not the first time they'd met and not when they'd had dinner at Cowboy's. That just sucked. Bo had taken an instant liking to Max when they'd met, but he'd assumed the man was straight. If he wasn't, he sure didn't seem interested in Bo.

"I'll do it," Max said in a rough voice as he looked at Bo. "If that's what you want."

What Bo wanted was to feel safe again, to not have ever been exposed to the hellish reality that someone could and would hurt him just because of who and what he was. What he wanted was to go back in time and stop himself from going to that club in San Antonio a few nights ago, to not have been so desperate to feel another man's touch that he'd nearly been killed for it. What he wanted was to know he wasn't damaged, but he was, and all because he'd been desperate and stupid and looking for a man who'd want him since the one *he* wanted wasn't interested.

"Bo? You want a roommate?"

Did he? Bo thought about how scared he was now when he woke up at night, how hard it was for him to even fall asleep. Did he want anyone else around to witness it if he woke up crying or panicking, trying to escape the assault that never seemed to leave his head? He looked at Max, saw the promise in his eyes. Max wouldn't judge him a coward if he woke up sobbing, or if he was too afraid to sleep.

"You," Bo whispered, the word scraping painfully over his raw and damaged throat.

"I'll go make the beds." Annabelle scurried inside. Bo barely noticed. He was so tired, and he hurt so fucking bad.

"I'll stay with you until you're ready for me not to," Max said softly.

Bo nodded as his heart did a funny flopping thing in his chest. Maybe he'd had too many pain pills. Or maybe it was just that he thought he might very well never be ready for Max not to be there.

* * * *

The dim light cast by the lamp on the nightstand softened the bruises marring Bo's face. It didn't matter, though — Max could vividly picture each injury the man had. The damage was more extensive than what Max had thought. When he and Rory had undressed Bo, Max had wanted to weep. Bo's slight body was covered in dark bruises and painful looking welts.

What had been done to him was inhumane, and the images of that battered body were what was keeping Max from being able to sleep. Every time he closed his eyes, he saw Bo, imagined the man trying to escape the fists and belts — Max knew what those welts were, he'd had plenty of them himself when he was a kid. Seeing those long, cruel stripes that had been pounded into Bo's flesh stirred up memories, which was never a good thing in Max's opinion.

A glance at the alarm clock told Max it was time for another dose of pain meds for Bo. Max gingerly got out of bed, trying to keep the bedsprings squeaking to a minimum. He nearly laughed at his attempt not to wake Bo — wasn't he fixing to do just that when he gave him his pills? But it just seemed kinder to wake the man with a gentle touch rather than the sound of metal grinding together.

Max palmed the pills he'd laid out and rose, walking quietly across the few feet that separated their beds. He knelt beside Bo's bed, worried he'd terrify Bo and bring on memories of the assault if he woke the man while lumbering over him. Max gently brushed a lock of hair off Bo's sweaty brow, letting his fingers linger on the soft, slick skin.

Bo shifted and moaned piteously, and Max thought his heart would break right then and there. He brushed his fingers over Bo's brow one more time then brought his hand to Bo's shoulder.

"Hey, Bo," Max whispered. "Time for your pain pills."

Bo's breath hitched and he turned his head towards Max. He lifted his arm and flailed his hand, crying out when his knuckles smacked into Max's chest. Max's stomach plummeted and he grasped Bo's hand with his, clutching it tightly to his chest.

"Bo, wake up, it's Max." Bo's fingers spasmed against Max's skin, right over his heart, then clenched tightly, catching a handful of Max's chest hair. Max bit back a hiss and leaned closer to Bo, trying to keep from having his hair ripped out. "Bo, it's Max, you need to wake up. C'mon, baby—"

Max jerked back at the endearment, wondering where the hell it had come from. He hadn't ever called anyone 'baby' unless there was an actual baby involved. Pain zinged out like a thousand tiny needles were spiking through his chest and calling Bo 'baby' suddenly wasn't so troublesome. *I should have slept in sweats and a T-shirt! Or a damned bullet-proof vest!* This is what he got for trying to make sure Bo felt comfortable! Max had felt awkward about being in just his boxers around someone else, but he'd shoved down his reservations because Bo wanted to sleep in his underwear only. He didn't want Bo to feel weird—or think *he* was weird. Plus Annabelle had thought the heat needed to be turned up for Bo's sake.

"Bo—" The fingers pulling his hair tightened and tugged. Max nearly toppled forward onto Bo in his attempt to keep from having a bald patch on his chest. "Bo, God—" *Damn it!* That hurt! The fingers causing Max's torment released him so suddenly Max flopped back on his ass. By the time he managed to scramble back up to his knees, Bo was pushed up on his elbows and looking at him with a mix of confusion and pain in his expression.

"What happened?" Bo rasped.

"Just clumsy," Max muttered. There was no need to let Bo know he'd damn near snatched Max's chest bald. "And it's time for your pain pills." Max handed the pills over then picked up the bottled water Annabelle had placed beside Bo's bed earlier. Max opened the bottle and passed it to Bo. Bo popped the pills and sipped at the water.

Max found his gaze darting between Bo's lips and the slow bobbing of the man's Adam's apple. He didn't get hard, but it was a near thing. Watching someone drink shouldn't have been a turn on, should it? Max didn't know whether it was wrong or not, but it was kind of sexy, and the only reason he didn't embarrass himself by tenting his boxers was because Bo was so injured.

"You had enough?" Max asked when Bo lowered the bottle from his lips. At Bo's nod, Max took the bottle and recapped it. He patted Bo's shoulder and started to turn back to his own bed only to have Bo grip his wrist. Had he forgotten something? Maybe Bo needed to go to the bathroom, or was hungry. "You need something else?"

"Stay…"

Max started to point out that he was right here, but Bo pulled him forward until Max's knees were pressed against the side of the bed. Well, it wasn't like he was going to sleep anyway. Max dropped to his knees beside the bed. If this was what Bo needed to feel safe, then Max would just have to camp out here for the rest of the night.

Except Bo had something else in mind. "Max, please…with me."

"What?" Max felt too many things at once, too many kinds of fear, but the strongest one was the fear of hurting Bo. "I can't… Bo I don't want to hurt you, and yeah, ain't either of us particularly big men, but that's still a small bed, and you're hurt and—"

Bo looked at him with those blackened eyes, and even through the swelling, Max could see the moisture building and threatening to overspill. Fuck it, he'd just have to be extra careful.

"Okay, baby, okay." Max didn't even try to stop the endearment from slipping free. "Let me come up from the foot of the bed, maybe that way I won't jostle you so much."

Max carefully crawled into bed and pressed his back against the wall, trying to give Bo as much room as possible. But Bo didn't seem to want room. He rolled to his side and faced Max, then scooted over the few inches that separated them and burrowed against Max. One of Bo's hands rested on Max's hip, and the other was pressed against Max's chest. Max wasn't sure what to do with his hands, but eventually he dared to let them rest atop Bo's, a move that set Max's heart to fluttering like a cage full of hummingbirds.

Sleep was definitely an impossibility now. Max didn't want to miss a single moment of this, because it felt so right to have this one man snuggled up close to him. And Max wanted this, he wanted more than this, actually, which meant he had some thinking to do. He couldn't possibly figure it all out in the few hours he had left before it was time to get to work—but it was a start.

Chapter Four

It wasn't the pain that woke Bo up, although he definitely was hurting. The nightmares that had been plaguing him since the assault weren't the cause, either. In fact, he hadn't had any dreams at all while he'd been snuggled up to Max. The feel of a stiff, fat dick pressing against his ass, *that* was what had brought Bo out of his pleasantly blank slumber. Bo considered himself a connoisseur of cock, having sampled plenty of them in his lifetime. There was no way he could sleep through a prime slab of meat stabbing at his butt, and no way he'd want to.

But even that didn't feel as good as Max's arms, one of which was cushioning Bo's head, the other draped over Bo's waist. Max's work-roughened hand was pressed against Bo's belly, low enough that the side was almost — *almost* — brushing the tip of Bo's cock where it was pushing past the elastic waistband of his boxers. One little shimmy, that's all it would take to feel that warm, sandpapery skin against his aching crown.

Bo didn't move. As much as he wanted to feel just about any part of Max touching his dick, he didn't want to wake the man. Then there were Bo's injuries. Moving at all was going to hurt like hell, and he certainly wasn't up to delivering on what he'd be promising if he did anything to encourage the man. And, even more of a reason for Bo not to wake Max, was the fact that Bo didn't know for sure whether or not Max was gay. It wasn't as if he had ever taken Bo up on any of his previous flirtatious offers. He hadn't slapped Bo down, either, but that could just be because Max was a nice guy.

The hard, hot cock stabbing at his ass didn't really tell Bo anything. Max was asleep, and he could be having some fuck dream about a woman, or several women — or maybe even about Annabelle. Rory's sister was cute enough, if one went for cute with boobs and a uterus.

That thought wedged itself solidly into Bo's brain. His bottom lip poked out in a painful pout — the damned thing was all puffy and split from a savage backhand. Bo bit back a wince and tried to scrub the vision of Max and Annabelle from his mind, but it wouldn't budge. After all, why else would Annabelle be staying here in the bunkhouse rather than in the big house with her brother?

But if Max and Annabelle were together, then why the hell was Max in bed with him? *Because Max is one of the nicest people I've ever met, and I asked him to. Doesn't mean the guy is interested in anything more, and just because his dick is hard doesn't mean it's hard for me.* Bo knew the truth of that, just like he knew he had a fine ass that had to feel pretty good to the heavy length pressing against it. He wasn't exactly vain, but he was aware of his attributes, and his ass was definitely one of his best.

Of course, if Max would just shift his hand down an inch or so, the man would come into contact with another one of Bo's assets. As if his thoughts had willed it, Max's hand twitched and nudged Bo's cockhead. The resulting zing of pleasure that shot through him made Bo tense, which in turn made him gasp as pain speared through his nerve endings.

Max murmured sleepily and buried his face against Bo's neck. His hand brushed over that sensitive tip again, and Bo shuddered as he hissed, unsure if the pleasure or pain drew the sound from him. Max snuffled and rubbed his dick against Bo's ass. The friction from that thick shaft thrusting between his cotton-covered cheeks felt so good, and went a long way to distracting Bo from the pain of his injuries.

At least it did until the arm around his waist tightened, stealing Bo's breath as his bruised ribs and hips protested the embrace. Before he could figure out a way to disentangle himself, and not really sure if he wanted to, Max ground his groin against Bo's butt and moaned.

If they hadn't been so swollen, Bo's eyeballs would have surely popped right out of his head when he felt the first spurt of wet, warm spunk seep through the back of his boxers. His heart thudded heavily in his chest as that damp spot grew with more proof of Max's release. As much as he wanted to be flattered, Bo knew Max wasn't aware of what he was doing. The man was asleep, and rutting against a damn fine ass, and probably dreaming about fucking some lovely woman. Bo refused to think about which woman that might be, choosing to think instead of how Max would react to this when he woke up.

Not well, that was the answer, especially not if the guy was straight. If that was the case, Max could have a definite freak out, and while Bo didn't believe he would be in any danger at that point, he still didn't want to experience such a scenario at all. And he really wanted to spare Max from any trauma. The man hadn't done anything except try to comfort Bo, and he shouldn't have to be mortified for it.

Bo only had one idea for how to prevent that, and he really wasn't too sure it'd work. Still, it was better than nothing. He just had to make sure Max didn't wake up before the plan was put into action.

* * * *

"Ffffuuuuuggh! God—" Max came awake in a hail of flailing arms and legs, kicking and swinging, his brain not yet capable of comprehending anything other than the sudden shock to his body. The back of his hand thudded against warm flesh. More cold liquid sloshed onto his groin right before something dropped down and slapped his cock and balls but good.

Max wheezed and tried to curl up, groping at his wet, wounded bits. His forehead smacked into something hard and angular. Pain spiked up his brow. Added to the throbbing in his balls was the clumsy groping of a hand— and it damn sure wasn't his own. Max yelped just about the time the synapses in his brain started firing. *Bo.*

Max's eyes snapped opened and he found himself looking at a kneecap covered in pale fuzz. He tipped his head back and Bo's concerned and battered face came into focus. Before he could ask what happened, his groin was scrubbed vigorously. Tearing his gaze from Bo's face, Max watched the man's bruised hand swipe at the dripping wet material of Max's boxers with part of the sheet. An opened water bottle lay in front of Max's crotch, spilling out the last dregs of the clear liquid.

"Sorry, slipped," Bo rasped out as he continued rubbing the sheet over Max's cock and lower belly. Max couldn't tear his eyes away from the image of that poor hand stroking his shaft, albeit unintentionally, and not in the way that Max wished it would. That particular part of him agreed, twitching and trying to harden. *God, no!*

"Stop! Just...stop," Max gritted out, reaching for Bo's hand. The last thing he needed to do was humiliate himself by popping a boner right now. And Bo certainly didn't need it, either. Poor guy had been through more than enough, and he had to feel like shit for dumping that water on Max like he did. Didn't he? A quick glance at the man made Max wonder—Bo looked...intent, amused, though with all the swelling and discoloration, Max could just be reading Bo's expression wrong.

Max clamped his fingers around Bo's wrist and tugged gently. "'S'okay, just leave it be." *Please, just leave it!* He fought to keep from tightening his grip as his cock started to fill.

Bo grunted and swiped at Max's waistband one last time before his hand stilled. Max started to breathe a sigh of relief as he looked at Bo. He had a split second to wonder at the grin teasing the man's lips, then Max's dick was caressed from root to tip. His half-hard shaft perked up fully and Max's heart nearly burst from his chest. Eyes locked with Bo's, anticipation and shame warred in Max. Jesus god, he wanted to *feel* Bo touching him, wanted to know what it was like to have another man's hand on his dick. *Not another man, just Bo. Just his hand on me...* But what would happen after that?

"B-Bo," he pleaded, not sure what he was asking for even as he spoke. He tried to determine if Bo was mocking him; it was so hard to tell with the bruising and swelling, but it was too late. Bo was cupping him through the thin, damp cotton, and now Max's humiliation was complete.

Or so he thought, but he'd never been a particularly bright person in the morning. The bedroom door flew open without any warning and Annabelle stuck her head in the room.

"Is everything all..." Annabelle's eyes widened so much, Max wondered how they kept from shooting out of the sockets. "Oh. Oh! I'll just...leave now." She started to do just that, her head nearly disappearing before she poked it back through. This time she didn't look so shocked, only confused and concerned. "Do you really think Bo's up to that just yet? He might be loopy from the pain meds. I'm just saying." Annabelle shot Max a narrow-eyed look before vanishing and shutting the door firmly as she did so.

"Ah, god." Max closed his eyes as his erection melted faster than a stick of butter in the hot Texas sun. His skin was burning with the intensity of his embarrassment, and all he wanted to do was crawl under the bed and hide for a decade or two. Spontaneous combustion would work, too. As if he hadn't been utterly confused before, he now had to figure out how to convince Annabelle he wasn't some dirty horny dog who couldn't control himself. She thought *he'd* started this? Had he? After all, he was the one who'd popped wood. Bo had just been trying to help...

"Max, don't worry about it," Bo whispered in his sandpaper-rough voice. "You weren't awake, and I was grabbing at you." Bo sighed heavily as if the words had cost him a great effort. Max knew they must have what with the damage done to the poor man's throat.

Before he could think of a suitable reply, the alarm clock blared. Max was used to the obnoxiously loud racket, but Bo, not so much. He squeaked and jumped and teetered at the edge of the bed. Max's hand shot out before he could think about it, grabbing on to the man's pale, lean biceps.

"I gotcha," Max soothed when Bo yelped again. "I ain't gonna let you fall." Keeping his grip on Bo, Max sat up so he could use both hands to steady Bo. Once he was sure the man wouldn't topple off the bed, Max gathered his dignity — there wasn't much of it left at this point — and scooted off the foot of the mattress. Water trickled down the insides of his thighs when he stood, which just felt a little dirty. It did *not* feel erotic or make him fantasise, not even for a minute, about something else running down over his skin.

"Damn it," Max muttered. At this rate he was going to be a walking erection. "Let's get you moved to the other bed, and then it's time for more pain pills for you." Maybe, if he had any sort of luck at all, those pills would wash the memories of this morning's events right out of Bo's mind.

* * * *

Okay, so maybe that hadn't been the best plan ever, but Bo hadn't been able to come up with anything better. He was blaming the crappy plan on the pain meds. Dumping his bottled water on Max had been a true act of desperation, and possibly just cruel, but it had been effective. Hopefully.

Bo lay on the dry bed and waited for the medicine to kick in. He was hurting all over, and Max had managed to knock the shit out of him, catching him in his sore ribs. It was worth it, though. Bo didn't know if it was the drugs, the pain or what that had kept him from noticing Max's sexy little body last night. He must have been close to dead, that was all he could figure, because there was no other way he could have ignored such a hot guy.

Max wasn't tall at all, but he still had an inch or two on Bo's own five feet seven inches. When Bo had noticed the man before—sizing him up the first time they'd met, because that's just what Bo did to men—he'd thought Max had an attractive, compact yet slender form. He'd kind of been wrong.

While Max did indeed look thin but toned, the truth was the guy was unbelievably cut. He wasn't bulky at all, just exquisitely detailed. Max's chest was covered with a thick dark pelt of hair, which turned Bo on in nine different directions. His pecs were still discernible, looking taut and tempting and topped with peachy-pink nipples. The groove running between his abs was deep enough that Bo knew he could drink from it—and he'd do his best to give that a shot, just as soon as he was feeling human again. And he really wanted to feel those hairy, muscled thighs wrapped around his waist—or his neck, hell, Bo wasn't picky. If he had been, chances were that fucker wouldn't have got the chance to stomp the shit out of him. But, no, Bo had been so lonely, and yes, horny, so he'd gone to a gay club in San Antonio, looking for something. The fact that he hadn't been able to stop thinking about Max had been part of it. Bo had been interested in the man since they'd first met. He had been careful during that first time they'd hung out, flirting a little and testing the water. Max had seemed totally oblivious to Bo's attempts to flirt, and that had been okay after a while because Bo had really just enjoyed the guy's company. A lot. Enough that he'd found himself thinking about Max often, more than he ever had any other guy. Of course most of the other guys in Bo's life had been one-night stands whose names he didn't bother with trying to remember. He didn't exactly really know them.

But there was something about Max...Bo had thought he'd give it another try that night at Cowboys. He had held out great hopes for once in his life not for a quick fuck, but for something more, something that would last longer, be more intense. Between thinking about the way Chance and Rory seemed so perfect for each other, and the way he'd just whored around and studiously avoided anything serious, Bo realised he really, really wanted a relationship, one that was special and would last. It scared him, but he wanted it. Bo was tired of running from commitment, running from himself, running from his past.

Of course his plans to seduce Max into loving him had backfired at Cowboy's. First off, Max had seemed as oblivious to Bo's charms as he had been before. The little flushes and stutters Bo had come to realise were from nervousness, not a raging attraction to Bo. Still, Bo had watched Max closely and noticed the man didn't check out anyone else—not the women in the place, and there'd been a couple who were pretty attractive, and not the men, who Bo would have catalogued as okay but not particularly impressive.

Especially not once Max had walked in. There was just something intense about Max despite his easy-going smile that drew Bo to the man. It made Bo want to giggle and act all coy like some teenage girl or something. It was that fluttery nervousness that had almost brought the dinner at Cowboy's to an end before it truly got started. Bo really hadn't meant to laugh at Max, he hadn't, but he had been so fucking nervous, and he'd laughed like a fucking idiot, and that right there had been the end of his plan to seduce Max. It had been all Bo could do to prevent Max from leaving at that point. Bo had been willing to do anything to keep Max there, but he was pretty sure throwing himself at the man's feet and begging would have only embarrassed Max more.

So Bo had been on his best behaviour, and once they had got past that uncomfortable situation, they'd got on like best buddies for life. Which hadn't been exactly what Bo wanted. Friends were all well and good, but he'd wanted that lover bit thrown in there too. And so he'd come up with the idea of having Max come to San Antonio and visit him. He'd figured that would give him time to work on Max, see if he was interested or not, because Bo hadn't been able to squash the hope that Max was interested and just really shy about showing it.

But Max had turned him down flat, using an excuse Bo didn't quite buy. He'd tried to shrug off his hurt feelings; it was after all entirely possible Max was a hell of a lot more dedicated to his job than Bo ever would have been. In the end, the answer was the same — Max wouldn't or couldn't come to San Antonio, and Bo had gone home and nursed his wounded pride along with that strange burning in his chest. That particular sensation got worse every time he thought about never having Max, and by the time Bo realised he didn't have some weird-ass heartburn induced by thoughts of Max, he'd already been trying to dance off the funky mood that had hounded him for days.

Even once he realised he was sort of really fond of Max, Bo hadn't stopped dancing. What was the point? Wasn't like Max was interested in him, but maybe Bo could find someone who was, at least for a few hours and pretend it meant more than just getting off. Pretend he wasn't settling, something he'd been doing for years but only then realising, thanks to his attraction to Max. Bo had set about putting on his most flirtatious manner, but every time it got right down to it, he'd felt off in some way he couldn't quite describe. Picking up tricks hadn't ever bothered him before.

Bo had finally got fed up with his own newly developed morals or conscious or whatever the fuck it was that was keeping him from getting laid, and he'd thoroughly stomped down everything but his body's need for release. He told himself to quit being so picky, to just take the next offer he got, but he'd already turned down most everyone who'd been interested.

When Bo had just about given up on finding *someone*, *anyone*, and was seriously considering leaving, he'd seen the man watching him. It hadn't taken more than a smile from Bo to have the big blond striding towards him. Bo remembered the shudder that had rippled over him then. Had it been a warning rather than the desire he'd taken it for? Probably, but Bo had been desperate to forget how alone he was.

As soon as the big blond was close enough, Bo had noticed the cold look in the guy's eyes. He had figured it for the disdain a lot of closeted men felt for their one-offs, or for themselves for seeking out another man. Well, he'd been wrong about that shithead, and it'd almost cost him his life. There was no use dwelling on that mistake.

There was another mistake he was thrilled about, though. Bo had been wrong about Annabelle and Max getting down and dirty. There was no way she'd have been so calm about walking in on Bo stroking off Max this morning if she was Max's lover. And Max had definitely liked the feel of Bo's hand on his dick.

If Max had liked that, then he'd love the other things Bo wanted to do to him. It was just too bad that Max would never love him. Nobody ever had, not really, which was why Bo was alone and miserable and looking for comfort in dark alleys and dangerous bars. He knew that, just like he accepted he was unlovable.

For all he knew, that might be because *he* wasn't capable of returning that tricky sentiment. Bo wanted to, he ached for that, to give it and receive it, more than he ached physically. It just wasn't possible.

But, for a little while, he could lie in this uncomfortable bed and imagine what it would be like to have Max love him. That's exactly what he did, letting those fantasies coax him into a dream-filled sleep.

Chapter Five

Max didn't know whether it was the rude awakening a few days ago, or the dream he'd had right before being doused with cool water, or maybe a combination of both. Either way, he'd had a difficult time concentrating since that rather chilly event. It didn't help that every time Annabelle looked at him, she had a smirk on her face that brought a flush to Max's skin. And he was almost certain she'd muttered that he had a 'really nice package'. Max was too afraid to call her on that. Between trying to avoid Annabelle and staring off at nothing, feeling alternating moments of mortification and arousal at the memory of having Bo scrubbing at his dick, Max was thoroughly behind in his work.

Then there was that damned dream he'd had the morning he'd ended up with a sopping wet crotch. Images from that dream kept popping up every chance they got. Visions of sliding his dick into Bo's beautiful ass, burying his shaft so deep the man could taste it, would flicker through Max's mind at the most inconvenient times. He'd dropped Rama's saddle then promptly tripped over it—and he'd *swear* that horse snickered at him for it—when a wave of sensual heat had rolled over him.

He'd just been minding his own business, doing his job then his brain had tossed up a vision of Bo's ass thrusting back against his groin, grinding and rubbing until Max had nearly come in his jeans. If he hadn't dropped the saddle, he'd probably have dropped his load. Taking a tumble was only marginally less humiliating than having his cock spew like a horny teenager's.

Now it was full-on dark, and Annabelle had gone to the bunkhouse to check on Bo. She'd given Max a wink when she told him she'd be dining at the big house. Max wasn't sure what that wink was for. He wasn't used to being around women much, and if Annabelle was a fair example of the opposite sex, they were just as confusing as hell. Maybe he should drag his heels and hope she'd be gone before he got back.

Max discarded the idea as cowardly as he made his way home. Wasn't like Annabelle was going to jump his bones—she just liked to tease, and that was something Max didn't have a lot of experience with. The fact that he really wanted to see Bo, only to make sure the man was doing better today, was an incentive to hurry he wished he didn't have to acknowledge. It scared him and thrilled him every time he saw Bo, and Max wasn't quite sure what to do about that.

Truly, the only time he didn't feel like a ball of ragged nerves around Bo was when they went to bed. After that first night together, Max had decided it'd be better to push the twin beds together. More room for them both if Bo had another nightmare and Max ended up in bed with him. Not that it made any difference. They always woke in the morning tangled together some way or another, usually right on the seam where the two beds pressed together. It was the most uncomfortable spot to sleep on, but worth it to feel Bo's warm body draped over his.

The porch light was on, which meant Max had to bat away a slew of June bugs and moths. There were other flying critters that he didn't bother trying to identify. Some things were best left unknown. The tarantula Annabelle had nicknamed Fred was hanging on the lower part of the screen door. Those hairy things were creepy as all get out, and even though they weren't poisonous, Max was certain he'd have a heart attack and keel over if one ever bit him.

Carefully edging his way to the door handle, Max kept a close eye on Fred as he slipped inside the house. Tarantulas could jump, and Max didn't trust Fred at all. He'd take the can of Raid to that spider—not to spray it, but to beat it to death with—if he didn't think Annabelle would have his balls for it.

Max breathed a sigh of relief when he closed the door behind him. Fred was still on the outside of the screen. He didn't have to worry about death by freaky spider tonight.

"Rough day?" The words were spoken with a painful sounding rasp.

Max yelped in surprise. Bo was sitting on the battered couch just inside the bunkhouse. This was the first time the man had really been out of bed, and he'd damned near managed to accomplish what Fred hadn't. Max's heart was pounding in his chest like it was trying to rip free from his body.

"You could say that," Max replied a little breathlessly. Bo was shirtless, which accounted for Max's asthmatic impersonation. It wasn't the first time he'd seen the man in such a state of undress, and it always did this to him.

Even badly bruised, Bo was still the most attractive person Max had ever seen.

Guess that explains why I was never much interested in girls. Women, excuse me, Ms Steinem. Doesn't explain why I ain't felt like this about any other men though. Max had thought he was asexual at the best of times, and a flat-out freak at the worst. He knew his childhood had screwed him up, especially his sexuality. After all, how many men reached his age and were still virgins?

"'C'mere," Bo scraped out, patting the cushion. A thousand crack-fuelled butterflies burst free in his stomach. It was one thing to cuddle with the injured man in the middle of the night, feigning sleep as an excuse to hold him close. This was more personal, a more conscious choice, and Max wasn't sure it was a smart one. That didn't stop him from tossing his Stetson onto the recliner and dropping down a few inches away from Bo.

"Looks like you're doing better today." Max swallowed his nerves and looked at Bo, noting the stark bruising on his neck and face. At least the swelling had gone almost all the way down. "Probably good for you to be moving around a bit."

"Bed's just no fun without you," Bo crooned in a rough voice that went straight to Max's balls. "I keep landing in the crack between the beds." Bo did something with his bottom lip, pushing it out in what Max thought might have been a pout. It looked painful with the healing splits scabbed over, and was more effective because of it.

"You could always lay in my bed," Max said, referring to the bed in his room. It wasn't much bigger than the twin beds shoved together, but the mattress was new and there was no man-eating crack in the middle of it. "I don't care if you do." He kind of thought he'd like that, actually, having Bo's scent on his pillows, secreted into his sheets.

Maybe even the mattress itself so that Max could lie there on lonely nights and catch the faint whiff of this man.

Bo smiled at him and Max was surprised to notice the man had scooted closer, nearly brushing against Max at the shoulder. "Thank you." Bo gave him a look Max wasn't sure how to interpret, but it threatened to set each of Max's nerve endings on fire. "I will probably take you up on that." Bo shifted even closer. His right hand gently rested on Max's thigh. "But in the meantime, I've got a proposition for you."

Max didn't know whether to be nervous or terrified. Once Bo had made his 'proposition', though, Max was actually relieved. He didn't mind sharing his bed with the man, and Bo had a point, it'd sure be more comfortable than sleeping in those twin beds. Max woke up every morning with such a bad crick in his back it was a miracle he could even move.

And if he was honest, there was more to it than just comfort. The idea of Bo in his bed night after night just flat out made Max happy, and something else — possessive. Not in the chest-thumping caveman way, but like Bo was his. It was weird, and probably wrong, but Max didn't want to think about it when Bo was smiling at him and just looking happy and relaxed. Then that smile dimmed a little before turning into a grimace. Max frowned and tried to figure out what he'd done wrong.

"You know what I was doing at the club," Bo said, his lids sliding down over his eyes.

Max grunted, confused as to why the conversation had gone from sharing a bed to…this.

"I have nightmares about it," Bo continued. "Not so much when I'm in bed with you, but I figure since I *am* asking to share your bed, you ought to at least know what happened that night."

Max's stomach dipped as he shook his head. He had to clear his throat before he could shove words past it. "No, you don't have to tell me anything. It's enough that you're here and you're okay. Well, you will be okay." He was screwing up what he wanted to say, but, damn it, he didn't want Bo to feel like he had to tell Max anything. "Really, you don't have to—"

"But I want to," Bo interrupted, lifting his eyelids enough that Max could just make out the irises and strips of white. "If you are willing to listen."

Max was willing to do whatever he could to help Bo, even if the idea of hearing what happened directly from the man made him feel a little nauseous. He didn't know if he could get through it without doing something humiliating like bawling or just as bad, losing his temper and cussing and hitting something. Not Bo, never him, but...

"I'd already kind of figured out I didn't want to keep fucking around," Bo began, closing his eyes again once Max nodded. He remembered Bo saying something about wanting what Chance and Rory had. "Well, I guess I thought it just wasn't going to ever happen for me and I might as well keep going the way I always had. I went into a club I've been in dozens of times before, but...it didn't feel right, you know? I was trying to convince myself nothing had changed, all I was going to ever have was a lifetime of one-night stands, but it just didn't...I wasn't into it."

Max thought that was one of the saddest things he'd ever heard, and combined with the longing in Bo's voice, it made his heart ache almost as much as it confused him. "Bo, why would you think you have to settle for that? Don't you know there's plenty of men who'd be happy to be with you—have a relationship?"

Bo snorted and grimaced. "Right, Max, and where are all these men, can you tell me that? Because I've not yet met a single one of them. And don't even tell me to look somewhere other than bars and such; it's not like that's the only place I've ever been."

Max bit his lip and was grateful he hadn't tried to tell Bo to look elsewhere. Bo had a point; after all, he'd met Chance on the rodeo circuit, and Bo had to have been more places than Max could ever imagine.

"So I'm at this club and I'm just not into it, but I keep hanging around because—well, it's what I've done for years. Then this one guy catches my eye. He wasn't exactly attractive, he wasn't ugly. He was just...there was something about him that kind of scared me. Sometimes...sometimes when I've been attracted to a guy, it's felt like that, like icy fingers tracing my spine and flicking my heart into high gear. So maybe I've picked dangerous guys before, or maybe I confused arousal with some internal warning system, I don't know." Bo shifted a bit and huffed softly. "All I can say for sure was, I was an idiot."

Max couldn't stop himself from reaching for Bo's hand. He cradled it gently as Bo looked at him. "No, you don't take the blame for what that asshole did. You didn't ask him to hurt you."

Bo's right eyebrow twitched. "Are you sure about that, Max? Maybe I like it rough."

Max growled as he gritted his teeth so hard his jaw throbbed. "I'm sure, but why you're trying to piss me off is beyond me."

Bo pulled his hand away and rubbed at his forehead. "I'm sorry, I'm sorry. You just seem to have so much faith in me and it's misplaced, Max. I'm not a good person."

Max didn't agree. Sure, Bo had to have made some mistakes in his life, maybe even a lot of mistakes, but that didn't mean he was a bad person. "I don't think it is. I think you are a good person. A bad one wouldn't judge him or herself as harshly as you seem to be doing."

"Right." Bo dropped his hand to his lap and leaned his head back. "Well, me, good person that I am, decided to let this crazy-eyed fucker lead me out into the alley, where he proceeded to pin me to the wall and choke me. I thought I was dead then." Bo shuddered and laid his hand on the cushion between them, turning it palm up. Max hoped he was reading it right, and he placed his hand in Bo's, relieved when the man's fingers slipped between his. "Next thing I know I'm alive and naked. And before you ask, no, the guy didn't rape me or anything like that. Turns out he was one of the bashers we all fear encountering. The only thing he did with my private parts was hurt them, either with his boots or his belt. I tried to fight back, I did."

Tears slipped down Bo's cheeks and Max couldn't stand it. He moved slowly but unerringly over until he could slip an arm around Bo's shoulders. Bo sobbed softly and turned into Max, looping an arm around his middle. "He wouldn't stop," Bo stuttered out. "Then he was choking me again…"

Max closed his eyes as he held Bo and gently caressed his back. He didn't let himself think about what he was doing, or why, all he did was hold Bo, and he'd keep on holding him as long as Bo needed him to.

* * * *

"What are you doing to Max?"

Bo jerked awake, the top of his head smacking into something hard and a little fleshy. "Ow!"

"Shit!" Chance flailed his arms and tumbled onto his butt. Only the fact that he managed to grab the wooden rail kept him from falling down the porch steps. Bo squirmed before he thought about it—his ass had gone numb. Maybe the bench on the bunkhouse porch wasn't the best place to take a nap. It was a little nippy outside, but the sun was shining and he hadn't meant to conk out.

Bo looked at Chance. The man appeared to be more than a little pissed off. "Sorry." Though really, Chance shouldn't have sneaked up on him like that.

Chance rubbed at his chin, glaring at Bo as he did so. "I shouldn't have gotten so close."

No shit. Bo rubbed at the goose egg on his head then let his hand drop. What difference did another bump make? He'd healed a lot over the past week and a half, but he still looked like cold shit.

"So." Chance pushed himself up but kept his distance. "What are you doing to Max?"

Bo forgot the advice Rory had given him the first time they met, about not trying to look cute and coy at his age. Glancing up through his lashes at Chance, he used his most innocent voice. It was a stretch. "What do you mean?"

"I mean, what are you doing that's turning my foreman into a bumbling, stumbling mess?" Chance threw his hands in the air then started pacing back and forth in front of the bench. "And he's bitchier than a momma dog guarding her pups. I swear, he'd as soon snap at you than say hello, and that isn't Max." Chance stopped and pivoted, facing Bo once again. One big rough finger extended out to point at Bo, and he figured he was lucky it was the index finger. "Max is all smiles and laid back and 'how ya doin' boss?' So what have you done to turn him into the anti-Max?"

Obviously the innocent act wasn't going to work. "I haven't done anything to him. I swear!" Bo tacked on the last two words to counteract the accusing look from Chance. Chance's face darkened with anger. *Well, now what? Why is it telling the truth only makes things worse?*

"Are you messing with him?"

Bo kind of was, but not in the way Chance meant. "I haven't touched him, except when we're in bed and —"

"What?" Oh damn, Chance looked like he might pop an artery. "What do you mean, except when y'all are in bed? I swear, Bo, I'm ready to..."

If Bo had to bet on what the rest of that sentence would have been, he'd have gone with 'knock the shit out of you'. Even though it went unsaid, he still couldn't keep from cringing.

Chance cursed and dropped down beside Bo on the bench. "Shit, Bo, I'm sorry. I didn't mean that."

"Sure, okay," Bo agreed, but he wasn't able to keep from flinching when Chance reached out to touch his shoulder. Chance went an unattractive shade of white, his expression guilt-laden. He couldn't feel any worse than Bo did about this whole clusterfuck. "I have nightmares about it." The words burst from Bo before he could stop them.

Chance made a rumbling sound beside him, but Bo couldn't look at the man, couldn't bear to see pity in his eyes. He kept his gaze focussed on his hands folded in his lap. "I asked him if we could sleep in his bed because the twin bed is too small, and pushing them together didn't work so well. I haven't done anything." Now Bo did look up at Chance, because if the man was going to get mad, this would be what did it—and it'd probably distract

Chance from the whole nightmare confession. "But I really, really want to."

Being good was driving *him* nuts, but Max was skittish as a virgin and those were something Bo hadn't any experience with. He could barely even remember losing his own virginity. Didn't want to, really, because he'd been too young and too scared.

Chance groaned and slumped down further on the bench, his broad shoulders scraping against the rough exterior of the bunkhouse. He pinched the bridge of his nose between his thumb and forefinger as if warding off a headache. "Bo, I don't even think Max is gay, okay? Maybe you should come stay at the big house with me and Rory."

Bo barely kept from stomping his foot and throwing a tantrum. It'd hurt way too much, and Chance would probably move him out of the bunkhouse in five minutes flat. He glanced around to make sure no one had managed to sneak up on them. Relatively sure it was safe, Bo turned to Chance. "He kind of rubbed off on me several days ago. Does that make him gay enough for you?"

"Oh god," Chance muttered and reached to rub at his temples instead. "What... How—no, no I don't want to know that one!"

Chance looked near to breaking, rubbing his temples so hard Bo expected to see smoke slipping between his fingertips. "So you're telling me that Max *is* gay, and that he, you know. On you."

The giggle slipped out without warning. Here sat a man who'd had his cock up Bo's ass and down his throat on more than one occasion, even if it had been years ago, and he couldn't even say 'rubbed off'?

Chance dropped his hands down to the bench and glared daggers at Bo. "It's not fucking funny, Bo."

"Yeah, it is," Bo teased. A flummoxed Chance was always sexy, and while Bo wouldn't poach—Rory would finish the job the man from the club had started if Bo even so much as tried to seduce Chance—he could still enjoy the view. "If it helps, he did it in his sleep. I dumped a bottle of water on him to wash away the evidence so he didn't die of embarrassment." He *so* could be thoughtful and considerate when he wanted to.

Chance's eyes couldn't possibly get any bigger. His laugh, when it came, was every bit as sexy as his confusion. "Oh damn, I'd have liked to see that!"

And just like that, Bo felt lower than dirt for sharing something that would absolutely mortify Max. "Don't laugh, he'd be really upset if he knew what he'd done."

"Yeah," Chance rasped out as he swiped at his eyes. "It isn't funny, I guess." He took a couple of shaky breaths then shook his head. "But that doesn't really count, if he was asleep. Doesn't make him gay, just a typical man rubbing his dick against something that feels good. Had to be your ass, right?"

"Like you even have to ask," Bo muttered, pouting just a bit. If it looked ridiculous on a man his age, oh friggin' well.

"I really think you ought to come stay with us before something happens and one or both of you gets hurt." Chance was using his reasonable, we're-all-grownups-here voice that always made Bo want to roll his eyes. But he could do mature.

"I want to stay here." So what if his mature sounded more like petulant? He was hurt, and now with Chance trying to force him away from Max, that hurt wasn't purely physical. Bo's heart actually pinched a little, and that was flat out scary.

Chance sighed, sounding extremely put out. "Bo, if he hasn't made a move on you, and you two have been sharing a bed…"

Bo had that one covered. "I'm injured, and Max is too much of a sweetheart to try anything when he knows it might hurt me."

"Yeah, maybe, but he'd tell you."

And that one as well. "No, he's really shy. You know that. I'd have to start it."

"He's probably cranky because he doesn't know how to tell you he wants his bed back."

Okay, that one hurt. Bo went back to staring at his lap when he countered it. This needed to end before Chance ripped his heart out along with his pride. "He wraps around me like a warm blanket every night—*before* he falls asleep. He pops wood every time we're in a room together. I've seen him looking at me, watching me from the corner of his eye as I strip for a bath. He's never had a problem with scrubbing my back. And what straight man would be secure enough to sleep with an obviously gay man, to hold him close and whisper to him when the nightmares come, to try to comfort and soothe—"

"All right, you win!" Chance snapped "He's queer as a three-dollar bill! I'm just not sure he got the memo, and he's headed this way, so we're done—for now." Chance stood and looked down at Bo, blocking his view. He really wanted to see Max. "You better fix him, though, not make it worse. I want my old foreman back. Yesterday."

Bo nodded even though he didn't agree. He liked the Max that held him at night and always made him feel like someone cared about him. Why wouldn't Chance want him to have that, to have what Chance and Rory had? Or did he just think Bo was too much of a flake to ever have a solid, loving relationship? Bo would have agreed not very long ago, but every moment he spent with Max made Bo believe he was worth something more than a fuck. Though he definitely wanted that, too.

Bo watched Max approaching, looking tired and dirty and oh so happy to see him. The man had a smile that lit up his whole face, and Bo's whole world. Maybe it was time for Bo to make his move.

Chapter Six

Max wasn't a hundred percent sure, but he thought Bo was up to something. The man had been sweeter than sugar to him for the past week. Bo was a nice guy, although Max was aware he had a bit of a reputation. He'd heard all about Bo's ardent but failed pursuit of Chance not very long ago. This went beyond nice, but it wasn't quite pursuit. He thought.

Every morning, Bo had somehow managed to wake before Max. The obnoxious blaring of the alarm was no longer necessary. Instead, Bo's soft hands kneading the muscles of Max's back was Max's new alarm clock. It was a better way to be roused from his sleep, even if Bo did occasionally let his hands dip a little lower than Max suspected they should.

Not that he was complaining. It just made his dick hard as a steel pipe, and maybe, when he thought Bo wasn't looking, Max rubbed that aching length against the mattress in tiny little thrusts. Bo never said a word about it, just massaged Max's back for several wonderful minutes—and yeah, sometimes a little south of there, too—before leaving Max alone and hobbling off to the kitchen.

Max had tried to stop him the first couple of times, not wanting Bo to strain himself, but Bo had just flapped a hand at him and...hobbled away. The erection Max had kept him from trying to talk the man out of it at that point, and besides, Max really enjoyed watching Bo's plump, pert ass as he made his way out of the room.

These morning massages had led Max to morning showers during which he jacked himself off. He'd been so reticent before to perform that particular action, always waiting for the wrath of God or his pa to come down and strike him dead. However, with Bo around, Max decided it was worth dying over. And it was either jerk off or die of blue balls.

There was lots of touching, accidental brushes against Max's hips, his ass, his hands, chest, shoulders, back—he didn't think there was a part of him Bo hadn't managed to lay a hand on this past week. Except for his cock—Bo hadn't touched that part of him since the whole cringe-inducing water bottle trauma.

Then there was Bo, teasing and laughing, bringing him coffee that he spilled half of before he handed it to Max. He'd also taken to packing lunches for Max and Annabelle, but Max's always had something extra, a candy bar or a muffin, something to take the edge off Max's sweet tooth.

The result was that Max was confused as hell. He didn't know if Bo was just being nice, or if he meant something more by all the attention he was giving him. It was driving Max nuts, because every little thing Bo did was a cause for his dick to swell, which permanently demolished Max's view of himself as asexual. He wanted Bo something fierce, but he wasn't quite sure what that entailed, or how to go about getting what he wanted. It was just flat-out hard to get something when you weren't real clear on what it was you were wanting.

Asking someone was out of the question. He'd rather be caught in a stampede of panicked cattle and squished into a puddle of guts and goo. The Internet was out, too, seeing as how the desktop in the bunkhouse was shared property. Max wasn't a total idiot—he had a damn good idea of what went where, he just didn't understand *how* that could go *there*! Christ almighty, that had to hurt. Only, if it did, then no one would do it, would they? Or not many people, anyway.

"What's got you frowning like that, Maxie?"

Oh yeah, there was that, too. Bo had decided to call him by a name that made Max think of a feminine hygiene product. That could not possibly be a good thing.

Max shovelled up another scoop of shit-covered straw as he tried to think of an excuse Bo would buy. Nothing came to mind, but that was mainly due to the fact Bo had stepped up right behind Max as he was bent partially over to shovel out the stall. Max could feel the heat from Bo's groin. The guy *had* to be standing with his dick a hair away from Max's ass, which gave Max's constant companion, Mr Wood, permission to try to burst from his jeans.

"Maxie?" Something kind of hard brushed across Max's butt when Bo spoke. Max thought about what went where and nearly leapt out of his boots trying to stand up and put a little space between them. All he succeeded in doing was stumbling, which resulted in Bo grabbing his arm and spinning him around. Max suddenly found himself face to face with Bo...and cock to cock.

Bo gave him a beatific smile and Max nearly creamed his jeans. "Is that for me, or do you *really* like the horse this stall belongs to?" Bo's eyes were twinkling, the thin skin at the outer corners crinkled into lines that Max wanted to lick. Surely that was not normal.

Max stepped back, his mind racing with not a single helpful thought. It was all in league with his dick, thinking about sinking into one of Bo's orifices. Max wasn't experienced enough to have a preference. He took another step back, slamming against the stall wall. Bo's smile shifted from angelic to predatory in the blink of an eye. Max found himself paralysed at the rapid-fire change as Bo began stalking him.

"Oh shit," Max stuttered out, not in fear, at least not entirely. His dick was beyond hard now, pre-cum leaking steadily from the tip. He clutched at the rough wood under his hands, trying to find something to hold him up because his legs were quivering, his knees knocking together.

Bo didn't stop until he was nearly on top of Max. When he spoke, his voice was lower than Max had ever heard it. "I've tried to be patient. I've tried being nice, being a flirt, being the perfect little househusband, dropping hints, dropping bigger hints, copping a feel, and yet you still haven't done one thing to let me know you want me. And I know you do." He reached down and rubbed Max's aching shaft. Even through his clothes, the touch set Max's blood on fire. It did absolutely nothing to help with his inability to speak.

"G—ungh!" Max thrust against Bo's hand, seeking more. Of what, he didn't care, he needed to come. His fingers scraped at the wood, then somehow, Max's hands ended up on Bo's shoulders.

Bo smiled wickedly. "I thought you'd never ask," he purred as he dropped to his knees.

* * * *

Bo had wanted this for so long, and he was terrified that Max would stop him if he gave him even a second to think about it. He had Max's jeans undone and shoved down along with the man's boxers in record time. Bo grabbed the base of Max's thick cock and sucked the fat dripping crown into his mouth.

Max yelped but didn't pull away as Bo let the bitter salty flavour roll over his taste buds. He tongued the wide slit, seeking out every bit of pre-cum he could find as he gently cupped Max's balls. He rolled the furry sac in his palm as he sucked Max's cock to the back of his throat.

Bo swallowed, knowing the constriction would demolish whatever control Max had left, and it did. Max groaned and fisted his hands in Bo's hair, then did what Bo had been hoping he would. Max began thrusting, holding Bo's head still, fucking his hard dick into Bo's mouth, into his throat. Bo fought the instinct to gag as he revelled in each push and bump, in driving Max this far out of his normally easy-going state. He loved knowing he had done this to and for this particular man.

Max started pumping harder, faster, and Bo sucked and laved, teasing the fat vein, the slit, the little bundle of nerves on the underside of the crown. Max was grunting with each thrust. Then as Bo slid his fingers beyond Max's balls to stroke the soft skin behind them, Max began gasping out Bo's name over and over.

Bo fought against slipping his fingers further back to tickle Max's hole, afraid that would freak the man out and end this perfect blowjob. He released his grip on Max's cock and grabbed a handful of ass instead. Bo's throat and lips were taking a battering, but it was the hottest thing he'd ever done by far. He returned his other hand to Max's balls and squeezed gently.

Max's thrusts became short and jerky as a guttural sound was ripped from him. His fingers were clenched and entrenched in Bo's hair, jerking the strands painfully as Max shouted and buried his cock deep. Bo felt the first warm spurt in his throat then pulled his head back despite Max's hold on him.

Hot bursts of spunk filled his mouth, Max's voice filled the air, and Bo filled his briefs, coming in his underwear like he hadn't since he was a kid. It was completely unexpected and definitely distracting since Bo had never climaxed without some stimulation to his dick, not when blowing a guy, at least.

Bo realised he still had his hand clamped on one sweaty butt cheek. Max was still trembling, hopefully from the intensity of his orgasm. Bo looked up at him and realised that wasn't the reason for Max's shakes after all. The man looked mortified, and angry. Those weren't the feelings Bo had hoped to inspire in him and his heart started beating double time as he tried to fight back panic. How had he fucked this up?

Sliding both of his hands up to Max's waist, Bo tried to figure out what was going on in the other man's head. Max refused to meet his eyes—his Adam's apple bobbed repeatedly as he stared at some spot above Bo's head.

If Bo didn't know better, he'd have thought Max hadn't been ready for a blowjob. But that wasn't possible—all men were ready for blowjobs pretty much all the time. With a sinking feeling in his stomach, Bo realised that all those men he was thinking about were the sluts he used to fuck around with, and yeah, he'd been a huge slut, too.

But Max...Max wasn't like them, or like Bo. He was the best man Bo had ever known, and Bo'd just kind of bulldozed the guy. Bo felt worse than he did right after he got the shit beaten out of him. How did he fix this?

He didn't know, but he damn sure had to try. He gently squeezed Max's waist, hoping to get the man to look at him. "Hey, Max? You okay there? I'm sorry if..."

Max swallowed loudly and jerked. He nodded and began pulling his pants back up, still avoiding Bo's gaze. He sidestepped, making it impossible for Bo to keep his grip on Max's waist.

"Max?" Bo couldn't help the squeak to his voice. He was utterly terrified. "Maxie? Can you tell me what's wrong?" He wanted to know how he'd so badly misjudged the situation. Max hadn't said no, hadn't tried to push him away or anything, and he'd seemed to enjoy the blowjob. Not that it was obvious now.

Max looked at him like he was crazy for a moment, then turned and walked out of the barn, leaving Bo on his knees and feeling like the biggest fuckup in the world.

* * * *

Jesus, what was wrong with him? Max nearly giggled at the thought. He was a damned mess, that was nothing new. And he was scared of the way he'd lost control and went after Bo like he had, shoving into his warm wet mouth and just pounding away. Actually, he was furious with himself for it. That wasn't the way he should have treated the man he cared so much for. Neither was running off, but he couldn't seem to stop. He'd had to leave before he did something worse, like push Bo to the ground and fuck him until they were both unconscious.

Max walked faster, his mind stuck on the fantasy of feeling Bo under him, the tight clench of his ass around Max's dick. He was so lost in the thought he nearly collided with Annabelle as she rounded the side of the barn the same time he did. Her surprised squeak was almost as loud as his, and she looked at him with startled blue eyes.

"Did you already finish the stalls?"

Damn it! What was he thinking, walking away from a job? Rapid footsteps distracted him and he craned his head around in time to see Bo hustling towards the bunkhouse, his slight shoulders drooping and his head tipped down. Max's stomach burned with guilt that he tried to hide. He didn't want Annabelle to know what a heartless ass he was.

"No, not yet," Max mumbled as he pulled his gaze away from Bo's slender form. He pivoted on his heels, his legs feeling strangely boneless. "I'll finish them now." Maybe shovelling more shit would keep him from thinking of the things he wanted to do to Bo.

Chapter Seven

"Bo sure took off in a hurry for an injured man."

Max grunted as he lifted the shovel full of nasty mess. It'd figure Annabelle would show up right after he'd had his brain melted. The best Max could hope for was that he hadn't lost the cells that controlled his power to speak — or not.

"Guess he'll be leaving soon since he's getting around so well."

Well, god damn it, how'd he manage to miss the fucking wheelbarrow? And why was Annabelle still chattering on, forcing him to think about things he didn't want to? Max glared at her from the corner of his eye as he started trying to scrape the mess up and toss it where it belonged. Annabelle wore *that* smirk, the one that told Max she knew something he didn't and thought it was hilarious. He gave up on glaring at her and concentrated on what he was doing, sort of. In truth, he was just trying to wait her out. She had to leave sometime.

"Smells a little funky in here." Annabelle made an exaggerated sniffing sound, her teasing voice stoking Max's irritation. It wouldn't do him any good to let her know that.

"Well, seeing as how I'm shovelling shit out of this here stall, I imagine it does smell 'funky'." Surely she couldn't smell anything else. The barn smelt like a manure-filled oven, thanks to the barn heater. Max sniffed cautiously — quietly — and didn't detect anything other than the usual.

Annabelle hummed and stepped in front of him, her expression far from teasing. "What'd you do to Bo?"

"Shit!" Shit, shovel, hay, it all hit the ground. "Annabelle, you need to let this be. I didn't do anything to that man." Adding on 'except lose my mind when he gave me my first blowjob, then I fucked his pretty mouth like some animal, rutting and shoving my dick down his throat' wasn't really an option.

Once he'd come, Max had been well past appalled with his behaviour. Bo had done something for him no one else ever had. Max had repaid Bo by violently thrusting into his warm, wet mouth over and over, battering away with no thought to whether or not he was hurting Bo. Added to that damning realisation was Max's pa's voice, dredged up from childhood beatings — not always his own — during which his old man screamed condemnation and threatened God's retribution for finding pleasure in the flesh. Max didn't believe the same hateful shit his parents had preached, but he still couldn't shake that voice or the judgmental words.

Annabelle stooped to pick up the shovel then began cleaning up the second mess. "Whether you know it or not, you did something, because Bo looked... Well, besides looking like he'd come in his jeans, he looked pretty damn unhappy."

As much as Max wanted to curl up and die from embarrassment, there were five words that seared into his brain: *he'd come in his jeans.* Max ignored the heat, from the heater and from the blood he knew had rushed to his cheeks. If Bo had come in his jeans, then that meant, what? That he'd actually enjoyed Max's brutal behaviour? Surely that wasn't the case. Maybe he'd... Max couldn't think of another scenario that would have left Bo with a wet spot right where it would have been in such a case.

"Think maybe I'll go talk to him after I finish this stall for you since you're all thumbs and dumbass today." Annabelle tossed a load into the wheelbarrow with more grace than Max had ever managed. "Unless you want to talk to him, being a guy and all that. Might freak him out a bit if I ask him about the barn smelling like spunk and horse shit, or the wet spot. Guys can be weird about that stuff if it's a woman asking."

Max knew he was being manipulated, and normally, it would have made him dig in his heels. Not this time. Annabelle was trying to shove him in the direction he wanted to go, and he really wanted to know about that whole jeans thing. And he knew he had some explaining to do. Max had been furious when Bo had been hurt, then he'd turned around and hurt the sweet little guy all over again.

Max heaved his best put-upon sigh. "Fine, I'll go talk to him. Didn't feel like mucking the stalls anyway." He walked out as quickly as he thought he could without arousing any more suspicion.

Annabelle's shouted, "Tell Bo I want details!" let him know he'd failed miserably, but he didn't care. Every step he took closer to Bo may have added to Max's confusion, but it also stoked the anticipation that was simmering in his veins.

* * * *

Bo ignored the knocking on the bedroom door. He'd heard the front door squeak as it was opened, recognised the sound of Max's footsteps on the wood floors, so he knew who was on the other side of the bedroom door. Maybe he should feel bad about Max having to knock—it was his room, after all—but it wasn't like Bo had locked the door, merely shut it before collapsing on the bed and curling into a ball.

Bo squeezed his eyelids tightly shut when he heard the door open. Max's steps were lighter now, so maybe the man believed he was asleep. The footsteps stopped then the mattress dipped as Max sat on the side of bed.

"I know you ain't asleep, can tell by your breathing."

Bo cracked his eyes open but didn't turn to face Max. "Annabelle sent you, didn't she?"

"I would have come on my own, just..." Max sighed. "Bo, I don't know what's going on here, and I hadn't ever...no one ever did anything like that to me before, you know?"

Bo felt his eyebrows crawling up to his hairline—which was still almost where it was twenty years ago. He flopped onto his back and studied Max intently, noting the deep red flush that tinted his neck and cheeks. The man was just too adorable, and too vague.

"You mean, no one ever gave you a blowjob before?" At the minute shake of Max's head, Bo pushed himself up on his elbows. This definitely bore deeper investigation. "You ever blown anyone?" Another quick, silent denial. "Been fucked?" Max jerked and a strangled sound slipped past his lips.

Oh shit. "Maybe I should have asked some of these questions before," Bo muttered. Although… "But you have fucked someone before, right? I mean, even a woman?"

Max turned an even deeper shade of red and stared at the floor. Bo's stomach took a dive to his ankles. "No one? Ever?" Bo whispered, not trying to be obtuse but totally unable to grasp the concept that Max had never done *anything*. "Did you even know…are you even gay?"

Max stood up and took two steps away from the bed before Bo could reach out to stop him.

"I'm sorry, Max, really. I just, I have trouble understanding how someone like you, handsome and so…just so *good*, could be a v—alone." Bo was sure Max would have melted into the floor upon being called a virgin, especially heaped on top of all the other questions Bo had just tossed at him. "I'm sorry," he offered again.

"I always figured I was just one of those asexual people, you know?" Max spoke so quietly Bo could barely make out the words. "Figured I was so fucked up from things that happened when I was a kid, bad shit that really messed with my head. Let's just say me and my brothers were taught, with a lot of help from a belt, that sex just wasn't allowed. Even holding your dick to take a piss could get us lashes that made it impossible to sit or lay on our backs for days." The bitter laugh that followed was so unlike the musical one Bo had started to treasure. This one sent icy fingers of dread skittering down Bo's spine.

"You don't believe that, do you, Max?" If so, Bo wasn't sure if he could or should try to change Max's mind.

"I don't," Max said and slowly turned to face Bo. "I know it ain't right, what my parents told us, what they did. But it's still stuck up here"—he tapped his head—

"and I don't know if I can ever get it out. If I can ever be normal."

The look he gave Bo was so wistful that it made Bo's heart ache for the man. "Do you want to?"

Max swallowed loudly, looking anywhere now but at Bo. "It didn't bother me too much before. I never felt like there was anyone I wanted to…to get close to." Max shivered once, twice, then finally locked gazes with Bo. "Then you came along, all smiling and happy, teasing me and being my friend. I started thinking about things, how screwed up my head was, how much I wanted to touch you, be touched by you…"

No one had ever said anything to him that had lit Bo up inside like those two sentences. He'd always been the good time boy, the pretty, easy fuck, just open an orifice, no need for anything more. And he'd never expected anything more, falling into the slot he'd been assigned by almost every man he'd ever had sex with. Then he found himself over forty and utterly alone and without a clue how to change that or his ways. Now here was a man standing in front of him, damaged as surely as Bo himself, and Bo had a choice to make. He could pack up his things and get out before he fell any deeper, saving himself potential heartbreak and a relationship that, if embarked on, would be a lot of work. Max wasn't the only one with issues. But he wanted to change, didn't want to be the man he'd been in the past. Bo wanted to be a better man, a good man. Except now he was faced with really doing so, it was a scary prospect. If he screwed up, he'd hurt the one person in the world who seemed to accept him and — Bo's heart fluttered in his chest — cared about him.

Bo looked at the kind, weathered face he'd become so fond of, the large, dark eyes, the nut brown skin lined and creased in such interesting places. Hadn't he been wanting something more than just sex? How many times had he imagined him and Max growing old together? Could he possibly have what he'd dreamed of? The only way he'd ever know is if he took a chance. After taking a deep breath, Bo held his hand out to Max.

"Would you like to touch me now, Max?" Bo held his breath, exhaling noisily when Max reached out and twined their fingers together.

"I'd like that very much."

Chapter Eight

It took every bit of Max's restraint to keep from diving onto Bo. Just the feel of his warm, soft hand, his fingers linked with Max's, brought to mind images of twined and tangled limbs. Max felt his dick swell as he sat on the edge of the bed. Bo was looking at him with so much trust in his hazel eyes, a soft expression on his handsome face.

A gentle squeeze to his hand gave Max the courage to speak. "I'm not sure what to do." It wasn't nearly as embarrassing to admit to as his confession moments earlier had been.

Bo's smile was sweet and hot at the same time. He winked at Max and shimmied where he lay. "Just do what you want. I promise you, nothing you do will be wrong. Just touch me, please."

The quiet assurance and the soft plea moved Max like nothing else could have. Something inside tightened, compressing his lungs, then loosened and fell away. The bands of guilt that had kept him bound vanished, and

Max felt a surge of desire so strong it nearly stopped his heart. He looked at Bo, letting the other man see the need coursing through him, saw the answering need in Bo's eyes, the pupils blown wide until only a thin band of green-flecked brow rimmed the black depths.

"Anything," Bo whispered, gently untangling his fingers from Max's.

Max felt a moment's despair over the loss of the touch until he realised he could replace that warm hand with other fascinating bits of Bo. Anything, he'd offered, but Max wanted *everything.* He skimmed his gaze down Bo's slender, sexy body, only then noticing he'd changed his clothes. The tight T-shirt clung to Bo's torso, emphasising the hard nipples threatening to poke through the material, outlining each rib and the concave stomach. A thin strip of pale skin was exposed between the shirt and the faded sweats. Max brought a trembling finger to that tempting bit of skin, marvelling at the silky smoothness of the pale hair that ran down beneath the elastic waistband.

Bo moaned and wiggled his hips, drawing Max's attention to the erection tenting Bo's sweats. As he stared, a wet spot appeared and spread. Max thought of what Annabelle had said, and even though he really didn't want to be thinking about it here at this particular moment, he had to ask. Max dragged his fingers down, feeling the heat of Bo's dick through the material. Bo's cock leapt beneath the touch and the damp spot grew a little bigger.

"Did you come in your pants in the barn?" Max found it easy to ask when he wasn't looking Bo in the eye and when he was touching that tempting cock even through a layer of clothes. Bo titled his hips, rubbing his shaft against Max's hand.

"You mean when I was blowing you?" Another thrust of his hips, a quiet moan. "Is that what you're asking? 'Cause, yeah, when you shot that first load into my mouth, I creamed my jeans, you tasted so good, and the way you fucked my mouth, just let yourself go and took what I was offering, oh shit." Bo shuddered and pumped his hips. "God, it was the hottest fucking thing I've ever experienced!"

Max forced his gaze away from the cock he was now cupping through the sweats, looking instead at Bo's face. There was nothing there other than lust, no deception or sarcasm, no anger at the way Max had ploughed into the man's mouth over and over. Even now, Bo's full lips were swollen, and Max was drawn to them like a hummingbird to nectar.

Releasing Bo's cock, Max shifted and leant down until his lips were almost touching Bo's. He wanted to look at Bo, look in those eyes that gave away so much more than Bo realised, but Max couldn't with the lush lips so close to his parting, a tip of a pink tongue darting out to moisten the plump lower one. A thrill of fear speared through him; he didn't know how to do this, how to kiss a man—or a woman, but that wasn't ever going to be something he needed to know. He only wanted Bo, this one man.

Bo licked at his bottom lip again, and Max gave in with a groan. He lowered his head, pressing his lips to Bo's, and groaned again at the heat that sparked and spread down his spine, slamming into his balls. Bo whimpered and buried his hands in Max's hair. His warm, wet tongue brushed over Max's lips, encouraging him to let Bo in..

Opening eagerly for Bo, Max shivered as his dick leaked pre-cum. He teased Bo's tongue with his own, and the taste of Bo exploded in Max's mouth, sweet and tangy, like chocolate and oranges, and something Max couldn't describe but knew he was now addicted to.

Bo sucked on his tongue and Max felt the pull all the way to his balls. He groaned and clutched at Bo's shoulders as he chased Bo's tongue, suckling it in return. He wanted to do that to Bo's cock, suck and lave that fat length, feel it push into his mouth, stretch his jaw wide and cover his tongue with cum...

Max broke the kiss, gasping for breath and trying desperately to keep his fears and insecurities at bay. He'd spent too much of his life being scared already. And Bo had liked it, hadn't he, when Max had taken over in the barn?

Max sat up and tugged at Bo's shirt. "Let's get these off, all of 'em."

Bo's lips looked thoroughly plundered but his eyes blazed with carnal hunger as he sat up and pulled off his shirt. Max zeroed in on the tiny peach coloured nipples with their thick pointy tips. God, he wanted a taste of those, too.

"You sure about these?" Bo rasped. Max dragged his gaze away from the tempting buds to find Bo's thumbs sliding under the waistband of his sweats.

"Oh yeah," Max ground out, his throat tightening with lust. Bo still hesitated, and Max narrowed his eyes. "Take 'em off."

Bo did this quivering thing, his entire body shaking bit by bit like a wave rolled over him from head to toe. He lifted his hips and shoved the sweats down his thighs, then kicked and twisted until he got them off completely. Max should have helped, but he couldn't look away from the heavy, fuzzy balls or the plump red crown smeared with pearly fluid, or the thick veiny stalk that he couldn't possibly swallow much of. Not yet, anyway.

"Max?" Bo's cock bobbed when he spoke, a fact Max found utterly fascinating.

"Yeah, Bo?" Max answered, watching a drop of pre-cum slide from the narrow slit and form a thin bridge to Bo's belly.

"Could you maybe..." Bo's breath hitched and Max hissed as Bo's shaft twitched. "Take your clothes off?"

Max's gaze jumped up to meet Bo's. "Oh yeah, I can do that." Bo gave him a hungry smile and Max quickly pulled his boots off and stripped. He didn't feel any of the embarrassment he thought he would have when standing naked in front of another person, not when Bo was looking at him like that, like he was everything good and perfect in the world. He just wished he knew how to live up to that look.

Bo rolled to his side and patted the bed. "Come here, honey. Tell me what you want."

Max lay down facing Bo, the affection in those warm eyes the only thing keeping Max from panicking over his fear of disappointing this man. Bo caressed his cheek, each stroke leeching the anxiety from Max until he felt nothing but the aching desire of moments before. Max wrapped his hand around Bo's left biceps and, using his weight, rolled them both so he wound up lying on top of Bo, bracing his body on one elbow.

"This okay? I ain't hurting you?" The full-body contact was firing all the nerve endings in Max's body, pulling his mind into a state of erotic bliss, but he needed to know that Bo was okay before giving in to his body's needs.

Bo thrust up, rubbing his cock against Max's, causing them both to gasp and groan. "Fucking perfect, Max. Please, do something, touch me, suck me, fuck me, God, something please!"

Images of each one of those acts spun through Max's head, maybe not in the clearest detail but it was more than enough to drive out rational thought. Max cupped Bo's jaw, loving the feel of the rough stubble against his palm, and took Bo's mouth in a kiss that left his head spinning. Bo whimpered into the kiss, clutching at Max's shoulders, his back, finally clasping his ass cheeks and grinding up while pulling Max's hips down. Their cocks were pressed together, slick and hard and aching, and Max couldn't do anything other than drag his lips down Bo's jaw. He nipped and licked, sucking hard on the firm column of Bo's neck as he began thrusting, matching Bo's tempo. Max buried one hand in Bo's hair, keeping his weight up on that arm while his other hand slid between their chests, searching out one of the peach nipples. Bo keened when Max's thumb and forefinger pinched the turgid bud. His fingers dug into the globes of Max's ass, pulling him down harder, faster.

Max felt his orgasm boiling up from his balls as his dick slid against Bo's. The head of his cock caught the underside of Bo's crown, and heat exploded inside Max. He tugged at the nub, pinching more from the spasm of ecstasy that caused his entire body to clench than from any intention. Bo screamed and bucked beneath him, spraying liquid heat between their stomachs. His fingertips brushed over Max's hole and Max didn't have time to wonder if it was intentional or not, that fluttering touch threw him right over the edge.

Max felt that first shot of cum spewing out like a punch to the gut. He howled with the intensity of his release, his vision wavering as jets of cum burst from his dick. He thought Bo's finger's feathered over his asshole again, but Max wasn't sure, couldn't concentrate on anything other than the ecstasy flowing from his shaft as he ground furiously against Bo's willing body.

When Max finally came out of his orgasmic haze, he was lying on his back with Bo tucked up against his side. Bo's head rested on Max's shoulder, and Bo had an arm and a leg slung over him. It felt almost as good as the sex had, or maybe as good but in a different way. Max glanced at Bo and smiled when he saw the man's sleep-slackened face. He was just too damned cute—whether that was appropriate for a man over forty or not, Max didn't give a shit, because it was true.

Besides being the sexiest thing Max had ever seen, Bo was simply adorable, a description Max vowed never to utter out loud. That was a little more…mushy…than he'd ever want to admit. Max's lids grew heavy and his last thought as he drifted off was that if this was going to send him to Hell, it was more than worth it.

Chapter Nine

The sound of the bedroom door opening startled Bo from the light sleep he'd dropped into. Carefully lifting his head from Max's shoulder, he cracked open his eyes and found himself blushing under Annabelle's appraising gaze as it encompassed his and Max's entwined bodies. The blush progressed from a subtle warmth to a scorching heat as he dimly realised he and his lover were both nude. Annabelle was getting an eyeful. Not just of Bo's fuzzy ass, either. He'd dozed off with one leg sprawled over Max's thighs and an arm draped low down on Max's belly. The result of this position was that Max's cock and balls were pretty much framed between Bo's limbs, setting those very fine parts of Max's body on display like an eye-catchingly framed painting in a museum.

Bo couldn't figure out how to rectify the situation without waking Max. The poor guy would be mortified to be caught all out by Annabelle. He gave her a pleading look and felt his own embarrassment vanish at the emotions flickering over Annabelle's face. Appreciation, curiosity, and desire melded into a thoughtful expression as she finally met his eyes. The pink cheeks were something he'd never imagined to see on Annabelle — she'd always seemed unflappable. Maybe it was just seeing two men together that had turned her on. God knew it would have made Bo whimper and beg to join the party once upon a time.

Annabelle arched a brow at him and tipped her head back. Bo didn't miss the way her gaze drifted over their naked bodies again as she waited for him to get out of bed. He mouthed at her to go wait in the other room, and she nodded once before quietly backing out, leaving the bedroom door open.

Bo gently lifted his limbs off Max in tiny increments, trying his best not to wake the man. When Max muttered and reached for him, Bo brushed his fingers through Max's thick hair and murmured soothing words until he settled back into a deep sleep. Once he was certain Max was out good, Bo eased off the bed and grabbed the sweats lying on the floor. He seriously thought about stepping out of the room bare assed. After all, Annabelle had certainly seemed to enjoy gawking at them, but then he remembered that flittering desire in her eyes, the hint of dawning realisation in their dark depths.

Definitely best to get dressed. Bo pulled the sweats on and grabbed Max's denim work shirt. The scent of sweat, horses and man encompassed him and Bo's cock sprung back to life. Bo buttoned up the shirt and breathed a relieved sigh at finding the shirttails hung to the middle of his thighs. He could still make out his erection pressing through the layers of fabric, but at least it wasn't quite so obvious. Bo closed the door behind him, cringing at the clicking sound as he did so. He waited, listening intently for a minute. When no sound other than a soft snore came from the bedroom, Bo smiled and headed out to find Annabelle.

She was waiting in the kitchen, sitting at the table with a sweating glass of iced tea in one hand. Bo considered getting himself a glass just to stall for time but Annabelle's gaze drifted down to his dick. After pulling out a chair, he checked the shirttail again then seated himself and scooted as close to the table as possible.

"You do know I'm gay," Bo pointed out, seeing no need to beat around the bush.

Annabelle snorted and rolled her eyes. "Well, duh. That doesn't mean the two of you didn't make a pretty damn fine picture."

Bo felt a burst of pride at the declaration. What forty-something man wouldn't? But he didn't want to appear vain. "Max is a very attractive man."

Annabelle chuckled as her cheeks tinted. "If by attractive you mean hung like a horse, I'd have to agree."

"Actually, I meant the entire package, not just his..." Bo fumbled through his indignation for a suitable word. "Not just his package, you know. I mean, inside and out, he's perfect even if he has issues and who doesn't? No one gets through life without some scars." Bo bit his bottom lip to keep from babbling. If he wasn't careful, he'd share more than he'd intended, kind of like he just had.

"I'm glad to hear you say that," Annabelle said, her lips twitching. "Max is a special guy, and so are you. I don't want to see either of you hurt."

Bo frowned before he could stop himself. He hated the way it emphasised the fine lines that had begun cropping up almost overnight. "Is that why you wanted me to leave that gorgeous man in bed alone, so you could tell me how special we are?" Women were so confusing. She didn't need to make him get up and leave Max just to tell him something he already knew.

Annabelle reached out and lightly smacked Bo's shoulder. "No, I really just wanted to get you out of the room before my big brother gets here. He wondered where Max was since he didn't finish his work for the day, and I thought I'd be nice and keep the two of you from getting caught going at it like bunnies."

Did bunnies have gay sex? Bo's frown deepened as he tried to picture that. He'd definitely have to Google the subject.

"Bo!" Annabelle snapped her fingers in front of his face. "Get your mind out of the gutter!"

"All right, all right," Bo sniped. "What did you tell Rory about Max cutting his day short?"

"I told him Max wasn't feeling so hot, and after whatever happened in the barn between you two, that wasn't exactly a lie. He was really shook up."

Bo detected the not so subtle probing and ignored it. "Okay, well, I guess we'll go with that. I don't want Max to get in trouble for messing around on the job." He hadn't thought about that. Max loved his work here and would be shattered if he lost his job. "I'll be more careful from now on, I just didn't think."

Annabelle shook her head. "Hey, no, it's fine for Max to have time off now and then, he's earned it. I just didn't think you'd want Rory knowing what was going on between you two."

"He probably already knows since Chance cornered me about this not long ago. He told me to get Max out of the funk he was in or move out. I don't want to move out." Not when he was fairly sure he'd finally fallen in love, at least a little, and it scared the shit out of him. No one had ever loved him, and he'd never loved anyone, not really, not like he wanted to. Bo knew he'd find a way to fuck it all up, but he still couldn't walk away. More info he didn't want to share with Annabelle.

"And why is that?" Annabelle asked as she narrowed her eyes at him.

Bo considered telling her the truth, but when it came down to it, if he really did love Max, then Max should be the first to know about how Bo felt, not their peeping Tomasina here. He wanted to make a smart ass comment to get her off his back, but whatever it was that was going on between him and Max wasn't anything he could joke about. Annabelle's sympathetic gaze made his chest ache. "I just don't, okay?"

"Yeah, Bo, that's okay. I think I understand." Annabelle patted his shoulder. "Why don't you take Max a glass of tea and maybe give him a little heads up so he can at least get some clothes on? I'm sure Rory's going to want to see him and make sure he isn't dying from some raging flu virus or something." She stood up to walk to the front door as heavy footsteps thudded up the porch steps.

Bo wished he could ask her what she understood, because maybe then she could explain it to him, too.

Chapter Ten

It had to have been the smell of cum that gave them away. Max burned with equal parts embarrassment and need. To be precise, he'd nearly keeled over when Rory had sat down and started grilling him about what he was doing with Bo. At first it'd just been a light round of questions, like was Max interested in Bo and was he sure that's what he wanted when Max had stutteringly admitted that yes, he was very interested in the man. That had been bearable, barely, and Max had thought they were done — but then Rory started asking specific questions. Max sat on the edge of the bed utterly stunned as the questions got more and more personal, like what had he and Bo done together, which had made Max blush so fiercely his blood must have been boiling right up under the surface of his skin.

Then it just got worse, with Rory talking about oral and anal and Max had finally found his voice and asked Rory what the fuck kind of pervert was he? Max was only now beginning to accept being pulled out of his asexual hidey hole. He absolutely wasn't comfortable discussing it, and that discomfort fired his temper into overdrive.

Rory had just looked at him with an arched brow and twitching lips, then started on a lecture that was close to thirty years past due. Condoms, safe sex, tests for diseases, and all sorts of things guaranteed to make Max just...want to die, right then and there. He'd only barely managed to shake his head when Rory asked him if he had condoms and lube — why the hell would Max have any of that stuff? He'd never used it when he'd jerked off. Rory had looked surprised, then at a loss and mildly embarrassed as he admitted he and Chance didn't use condoms, therefore he couldn't give any to Max. Max wanted to snark something about Rory practicing what he preached, but for all Max knew Rory and Chance had already done all that testing stuff and Max would end up looking like an even bigger idiot.

Rory had hollered for Bo, and the instant that sexy man walked into the room Max found the heat of embarrassment shifting to a different sort of heat, this kind slithering down to Max's cock and settling in his balls. It was a reaction Max couldn't hide, sitting there with his legs spread and only the thin sheet covering his parts. Rory had coughed, one of those 'disguise the laughter' kinds of coughs, which Max had chosen to ignore. He hated to be laughed at, but he was too mortified by what Rory had been talking about to care that the man was snickering at him now.

"You have condoms and lube, or do I need to pick some up for y'all tomorrow when I'm in town?"

Bo didn't even blink at Rory's question. Instead his eyelids dropped down as he shot Max a look that had him biting back a whimper. "I have some, though we're probably going to need more. Soon." Bo glanced from Max to Rory, then back at Max. "Has he been giving you a hard time, Maxie? You're looking a little tight through the shoulders."

Max ignored Rory's snigger when Bo called him Maxie. As far as Max was concerned, Bo could call him whatever he wanted when Bo was looking at him like he wanted to eat him up one slow, sweet bite at a time. Max cleared his throat and rolled his shoulders, chasing off some of the tension that had settled there during Rory's lecture. "I'm fine. Just going through sex ed all over again." Well, really for the first time. His parents hadn't allowed any of their children to be taught anything about sex other than it'd send them straight to hell. That wasn't something he was ready to share, especially with Rory sitting there with a shit-eating grin on his face.

Irritation snapped in Bo's eyes and his voice as he looked at Rory. "I wouldn't do anything to put him at risk. When I was in the hospital, they ran every damned blood test known to man and everything came back fine. I may have been a slut, but I was always a careful one."

Okay, Max had sort of known Bo wasn't exactly a prude, but a slut? Max had to think about that for all of two seconds. He didn't want to think about any man touching Bo, but Max was realistic and couldn't see where he had any right or reason to be jealous. He was a little concerned, though, about why Bo had ever thought of himself as a slut, or why he'd done things to make himself fit into that role. Max was absolutely determined Bo would never think so little of himself again.

Max had been so lost in his own thoughts he'd barely heard the drone of conversation between Bo and Rory. Whatever was said, the two men seemed to have got past the flare of temper from moments earlier. Rory stood and patted Max's shoulder before exchanging goodbyes and leaving. Max forgot the humiliating conversation with Rory. Nothing could compete with the ache building inside him for one very special man.

And that man was looking at him with a heated gaze that made it nearly impossible for Max to breathe. There was desire in that look, sure enough, but there was something softer that sent warm tendrils of effervescent hope through Max. "Lay back and kick off that sheet," Bo ordered.

Max swallowed and bobbed his head, unable to look away from the erection tenting Bo's sweats. "Yeah, yeah, okay." He flopped back on the bed, still keeping his eyes on Bo's bulge.

Bo shuffled over to the duffle bag he'd set in the corner by the dresser. He crouched down and dug out something then stood back up. With his back to Max, Bo stripped, his hips swaying slightly as he shoved his sweats down. Max's gaze zeroed in on Bo's pert ass, drinking in the sight of those firm globes and the dusky crease separating them. By the time Bo stood up straight and turned around, Max's cock was leaking pre-cum at a steady rate.

Bo started moving, a sensual swivel of hips and dick that freed the whimper Max had bitten back earlier. Max held out a hand to his lover. "C'mon over here."

Humming, Bo stalked Max, moving slow and pinning Max with his gaze. Max struggled to think. There was something he wanted to make clear.

"You aren't a slut." Not now, not ever.

Bo's step faltered but he quickly recovered. "Used to be. There's plenty who'd still say I am."

Max would beat their heads in if they did. "But you're not." Max levelled his lover with a look that he hoped was sexy and powerful and everything he wanted to be for Bo.

"I don't care about what happened in the past. All that matters is here, now, us—and you knowing what you are." Bo had completely stopped walking now. He looked sad and hopeful and terrified all at the same time. He started to speak, but Max waved him off with a hand slicing through the air. "There's only one thing you need to believe is true about who and what you are right now."

"Oh really?" Bo asked neutrally. "And what is that?"

Max shoved off the bed and was up and pressing against Bo's chest in a split second. He kept one arm around Bo's hips and with the other he grabbed a handful of the silky fine hair. Max didn't have gentle in him just then and he took Bo's mouth in a kiss that threatened to bust both their lips. By the time Max felt he had thoroughly claimed Bo, or his mouth at least, Max was ready to shoot his load. He leaned in and nipped a tempting patch of skin on Bo's neck before trailing kisses up to Bo's ear while he shuddered in Max's arms.

"The only thing you need to know and believe"—Max nudged his dick against Bo's—"is that you. Are. Mine."

* * * *

Bo had every intention of putting the condoms he'd grabbed to good use, but hearing those words from Max had rocketed him right to the edge of a climax. No one had ever wanted him, claimed him like that. Condoms flying every which way, Bo tackled Max, taking them both down onto the bed. Almost before hitting the mattress, they were rubbing off on each other in a frenzied burst of heat. In mere minutes their bellies and chests were covered in cum, their hearts racing and the only sound in the room was the rasping rattle of their breaths.

Bo had fallen asleep, sticky and sated and more content than he'd ever thought possible, and he had a plan in place for getting Max's thick cock in his ass first thing in the morning. The thing about plans, though, at least in Bo's experience, was that they tended to get altered by outside forces.

The first outside force was Sheba, a pretty bay mare who dropped her foal in the middle of the night. Of course it wasn't an easy birth, but hours later when that little baby straggled to his feet, his thin legs wobbling, even Bo couldn't be irritated about the change in plans. Bo had felt a warm fluttering in his chest when he watched the newborn take his first steps, and pushed his plans back a few hours.

Then there'd been the downed fence in the south pasture. By the time Max straggled in that night it was almost eleven, and he had looked ready to drop where he stood. Bo had shelved his own needs and taken care of Max, who'd been too exhausted even to stay awake during the shower they'd shared. He told himself it would be enough just to sleep with Max, to feel the man pressed against him and listen to his soft snores, and it had been — for the whole three hours Max got to sleep.

Another mare, another foal, and so it continued. Four days had passed without Bo and Max being able to do much more than kiss each other goodnight if they were lucky, and Bo had had enough. He needed Max to touch him. Even with the logical reasons for the frenetic pace around the ranch lately, Bo illogically felt as if Max was avoiding him. Nothing he told himself could chase that feeling away, and Bo was desperate to be reassured that he was still Max's. He didn't want to lose what he'd always wanted, not now and not before he ever truly had it.

Bo sat on the couch, trying his best to come up with a solution that didn't involve him jumping Max while the man slept. It wasn't looking good—unless he could get some help. *That* he could do, and he knew just who to ask.

Chapter Eleven

"You sure you're up to this? It's kind of chilly out."

Bo arched a brow at Annabelle and tried not to give a raunchy reply about how Max would be warming him up soon.

Annabelle arched a brow right back, and damned if she didn't do it better, too. "I meant riding out to Max. You're still moving a little stiff—don't *even* say it, Bo, or I'll insist on riding along and keeping y'all company. That might put a damper on your plans."

"At this point, I don't think so," Bo muttered, ignoring the blush those words brought to Annabelle's cheeks. "Nothing short of the apocalypse is going to stop me this time—and even that might go unnoticed if things go right. But thanks for your help."

Annabelle snorted and slapped Bo on the ass as he mounted his horse. "You deserved that, so don't even give me that wounded look. Got everything y'all need?"

Bo felt his cheeks—the ones on his face and the one Annabelle had walloped—warming up. Maybe he was just paranoid after Rory's little chat with Max, but it seemed like she was getting way too close to a safe sex talk for his comfort. "Yep, got it. Gotta go!" Bo reined his mount around and took off, almost as eager to escape Annabelle as he was to find Max.

Half an hour later, Bo halted his horse and looked around the area Annabelle had suggested. The stream that ran through this part of the ranch was full, the current moving at a steady clip, the sounds of water flowing almost musical. There was plenty of shade, the grass was green and not too high, and there wasn't another soul around. Not yet, at least.

Bo dismounted and led his horse to the stream for a drink. Once that was taken care of, he tied the horse to a sturdy branch in a good sized patch of shade and went to work setting up. Pulling the blanket roll from the saddle bag, Bo tried to decide the best spot to put it down. Somewhere away from the horse, for certain.

There was a perfect place beside the stream, a nice sunny patch where they could lay after and hopefully not get chilled. Bo spread the blanket down then hurried back to grab the lunch he'd pack for him and Max along with the condoms and lube. He placed it all on the blanket then hesitated. Should he strip down now, or wait until Max had eaten? The sound of hoof beats sent a shiver down Bo's spine. His dick was so hard that he hurt clean up to his belly button. *Oh hell, we can both work up more of an appetite.* Bo stripped out of his clothes and sprawled out on the blanket and only then thought of the shit he'd catch if that wasn't Max he heard approaching.

This plan was definitely holding together better than his first one, because Max rode right up to the blanket and seared Bo with a heated look.

"I was wondering why Annabelle told me to get my ass over here," Max rasped, his gaze trailing down to Bo's cock. "I was gonna come up to the bunkhouse for...but this is better."

Bo's mouth went dry as Max dismounted. He wished he could say something witty or seductive, but his throat was too tight, his breath too short. Max didn't even tie off his horse, just nudged its shoulder with his and told it to 'go on home' as he visually devoured Bo.

A tendril of fear slithered through Bo. This felt more intense than he'd ever imagined, more...just *more*. He realised, as Max began removing his own clothes, that something irrevocable and life-altering was about to happen. As much as he wanted it, wanted to love and be loved, he hadn't known it would be such a scary thing to experience. It dawned on Bo that Max could crush him with a few words — *no, leave, whore* — not that he thought Max would ever call him names, but it wouldn't exactly be an untruth.

Max took off his boots, grunting then grumbling about needing his damn boot jack, then he shoved his jeans and boxers down and Bo forgot to be worried. The sight of that fat cock slapping against Max's stomach brought the liquid back to Bo's mouth, making it water as he hungered for a taste of the pre-cum beading at the slit. Max shrugged out of his shirt then fisted his shaft, pumping it leisurely despite the passion simmering in his eyes. Bo quivered as he trailed his gaze over Max's enticing form. Broad-shouldered and leanly-muscled, he was the epitome of male perfection, everything Bo could have asked for in a lover, and Bo needed Max now before his doubts and fears could claw back to the surface.

Propping up on one elbow and clutching the blanket, Bo felt for the lube with his other hand. His fingers brushed against the plastic bottle just as Max let go of his dick.

"Let me," Max ordered softly as he stepped onto the blanket. Bo nodded and pulled his hand back. "Spread your legs wider."

Bo had spread his legs for more men than he could count and never so much as thought twice about it—even though he should have. But something about Max's expression, the wonder and hunger, the way he looked at Bo as if he were the most perfect gift Max had ever been given, brought a warm flush to Bo's skin. It was humbling and intoxicating at the same time, and Bo felt more than a little shy as he bent his knees and parted his legs, opening himself for Max's viewing.

Max sucked in a rattling breath and knelt on the blanket, his knees only inches from Bo's ass. "Look at you," Max murmured as he trailed his fingertips over Bo's lightly furred thigh. "Ain't a part of you that ain't perfect."

Bo knew better. If he'd been perfect, his mother wouldn't have ran off and left him to die when he was a baby. He wouldn't have been passed around and told what a burden he was by family members who took him in only to keep from looking bad. He wouldn't have let men use him just to feel like someone cared for a few minutes. He wouldn't have got the shit beaten out of him for being stupid and lonely and scared of both of those emotions.

But he couldn't say any of that, not when Max was looking at him like that, not when Max was touching him, smoothing his hand over Bo's stomach, his fingers teasing at the crease where Bo's thighs and torso joined. All Bo could do was shiver and moan and thrust his hips as he tried unsuccessfully to get Max to touch his aching cock.

"Please, please, Max!" Any other time Bo might have cringed to be so needy, but he couldn't do anything else, couldn't think or plan or measure his words. "I need you, aching for you—"

"You got me." Max leaned over Bo and grabbed the lube. Bo took advantage of the position to wrap an arm around Max's waist and pull himself up to suck at Max's nipple. He laved the nub, loving the surprisingly soft hair that circled the sweet flesh, the way it tickled his upper lip. Max hissed and palmed the back of Bo's head, pulling him closer. Bo took it for the demand it was and nipped the erect bud, rolling it gently between his teeth. He pinched and twisted the other nipple, mimicking the movements of his mouth, teeth and tongue as best he could. Max's fingernails bit into Bo's scalp, a little twinge of pain, as Max moaned and pressed into Bo's ministrations.

"Enough or I'm gonna come all over you," Max threatened, spacing his words out between gasps. He loosened his hold on Bo and leaned away, forcing Bo to give up the tasty treats he'd been enjoying.

Bo laid down and grabbed the back of his thighs, pulling his legs up to his chest. "Another time. Right now I need you to fuck me."

Max's expression turned thunderous and he stopped pouring the lube into his cupped hand. He glared at Bo with so much anger that Bo squirmed. "It ain't fucking, are we clear?"

Ashamed of himself, Bo nodded. He should have known Max wouldn't care for that, not yet at least. "I'm sorry, I'm not used to…" …*it being anything more than fucking.* "I'm sorry, okay? You're right." *Now please, hurry up!* Bo did his best to plead with his eyes, his mouth, his body. Max gave him a look that said they'd be discussing what Bo wasn't used to in the near future.

Max dipped his fingers into the lube he'd squirted into his hand then hesitated, all of a sudden looking nervous. "I don't want to do this wrong," he confessed.

Bo thought it was sweet and wanted to tear his own hair out. "Max...please, either do it or let me. You won't screw up, I promise, just make sure there's plenty of lube then...*ahh! Ohmygod!*" The feel of Max's fingers pushing into his ass nearly made Bo blow his load. The nerve endings in the tight ring of muscles pulsed with ecstasy, sharing it with his balls and every cell in Bo's body.

"Is that a good *ohmygod* or a bad one?" Max asked as he began to withdraw his fingers, looking at Bo worriedly.

Bo let go of one of his thighs and grabbed Max's wrist to keep him from pulling all the way out. "That's an *I'm gonna die if you don't hurry up and f—finish this!*"

Max grinned and began stretching Bo again. His fingers grazed Bo's prostate and Bo jolted, squeaking as he struggled not to come. Max's grin widened and his eyes took on a wicked gleam as he bumped that spot again.

"*Unngh!* Max!" Bo nearly swallowed his tongue the next time his gland was stroked. His stomach tightened as his hole clenched and rippled around Max's fingers.

Max's eyes shot wide open and he moaned. "I've got to feel that on my...on my dick." He pulled his fingers out and leaned over Bo again, reaching for and snagging a condom.

"Hurry, hurry, hurry," Bo babbled, "need you so bad, need to feel you in me, you said I was yours—"

Max ripped open the package and slid the condom on with minimal fuss. He lined his cock up and locked gazes with Bo. "You are mine, and I'm yours." Max gripped Bo's ankles and brought his legs to rest on Max's shoulders. "Look at me," Max ordered, sliding his hands down Bo's thighs.

Bo hadn't realised he'd closed his eyes until then. He opened them and Max gave him a wicked smile. His fingers tightened, digging into Bo's muscles in an exquisite way. Max pressed forward slowly and steadily, forcing the fat crown into Bo's opening. Bo's eyelids fluttered even as he cried out with the sheer pleasure of feeling Max entering his body. "More, please, Max!" Bo pleaded, needing everything Max had.

Max growled and snapped his hips, fully seating his dick in Bo's ass. There were gasps and moans, and Bo didn't know whose was whose and didn't care because Max began thrusting, long, deep strokes into Bo's needy channel countered by slow withdrawals that stretched Bo's hole open wide on the crown of Max's cock. Bo reached down to fist his own shaft as a blinding ecstasy zinged through his body and filled him until he thought he would pass out. Max grunted and began thrusting harder and faster, filling Bo with his thick shaft over and over.

"*Bo!*" Max's cock swelled inside him as Max ground against his ass. Max released a guttural groaning sound from his throat that sent shivers of desire straight to Bo's balls. Bo felt the cum spurt from Max's dick into the latex, and that shot Bo over the edge, screaming as spunk sprayed from his cock onto his chest and belly. His muscles cramped with the intensity of his climax, his vision blurred and became a thousand dots of rainbow colours.

Max thrust one more time, then lowered Bo's legs from his shoulders. He dropped down onto Bo, catching his weight on his forearms. Max kissed him languidly, soundly, and Bo kissed Max back with every bit of love he'd always wanted to give and never been able to.

It was the most perfect moment in Bo's life, and he knew he'd carry it close to his heart for as long as he lived.

Chapter Twelve

Dinner was ready, the table was set, and it looked pretty damned romantic if Max did say so himself. After the humiliating experience of asking Annabelle *how* to make this a special evening, it damn sure better look romantic. Once she'd made a couple of lewd suggestions, which had nearly given Max a coronary, she'd actually been really helpful.

However, next time Max would just Google any question he had. At least the search engine wouldn't start tossing out suggestions for positions in an ungodly innocent sounding voice.

Max lit the candle just as he heard Chance's truck pull up. The diesel engine had a particular grind to it that made it easy to recognise. Max felt his calm shatter a little. Sweat broke out on his brow, his upper lip, his palms... *Oh, fuck*! He was going to stink to high heaven before Bo even got through the door!

The truck doors slamming shut lit a fire under Max's feet. He sprinted for the bedroom, his boot heels smacking the hardwood floor hard enough that Max figured he might just have left dents. He grabbed the body spray Annabelle had gifted him with — which he'd muttered over the uselessness of in the safe confines of his room. After a few sprays of the stuff, Max tossed the can in the vicinity of the dresser and hurried into the living room without a second to spare. Bo was already pulling the screen door open.

"How'd the doctor appointment go?" Max asked, moving forward. He reached for Bo, noting the strain around the man's eyes. "You okay?"

"Just tired." Bo leaned against him as Max embraced him. He rested his head on Max's shoulder and sighed as he lightly gripped Max's hips. "You feel so good. Smell good, too."

"Ah, how did...what did the detective have to say?" Max struggled to concentrate. Besides the doctor appointment, Bo had had a meeting with the detective handling his assault case. So far, last he'd heard, the cops didn't have a fucking clue who the man was who'd hurt Bo.

And it didn't seem like that had changed. "She didn't say much of anything. Nothing new, anyways. No clues, no nothing, no one saw us leave together."

Max growled and tried to tamp down his anger. "How the hell did no one see y'all leave? There were other people there, right?"

Bo snorted and nodded. "Yeah, but that's just it. Place like that is crowded and the men there aren't paying attention to anything except their next piece of ass. Believe me when I tell you people there most likely did *not* notice me and Psycho Fucker slipping out together."

Max couldn't imagine anyone not noticing Bo, but arguing would just upset the man and he'd looked tired when he'd come in. Max let it drop, although he did ask, "So what are the cops doing then?"

"What can they do?" Bo asked in return, shrugging. "It sucks, but not every crime is solved like they are on TV. Looks like the bad guy is going to get away this time, which is really shitty because what if next time he kills someone? And there's nothing I can do. I even called the club I was at that night and asked if they'd hand out flyers or something telling people to watch out for the guy, and the owner refused. Didn't want to risk scaring off any customers."

"Son of a bitch," Max muttered. "He put money before someone else's life?"

"*She*," Bo corrected. "And there's plenty of people like that in this world."

Max couldn't disagree, but there were plenty of good people too, which he pointed out to Bo before dropping the subject like Bo seemed to want. Judging by the way the man was nibbling at Max's lips, he didn't think Bo wanted to talk much at all. "Bo—" Max whimpered as Bo burrowed against his neck and licked a strip up to his ear. Bo sucked on his earlobe and Max felt his knees tremble. Two weeks of making love hadn't done a thing to douse the desire between them. Still, as badly as Max wanted to bend Bo over the couch and plough into his hot, silky ass, he was determined to romance his man tonight. That didn't exclude the couch, just postponed it for a bit, Max promised his disappointed dick.

"The doctor said I'm good to go, healthier than a lot of men 'my age'." Bo sneered the last two words, clearly miffed. Max thought his vanity was rather cute. He'd managed to talk Bo out of dying over the streaks of grey hair—on his head—and there'd been a whole different discussion when he'd walked in the bathroom and found Bo getting ready to wax off his body hair. Max had convinced him, both times, with some very ardent love making, that grey hair was sexy. Besides, as he pointed out, Bo sure didn't seem to mind Max's grey at all. He hadn't, however, even bothered trying to talk Bo out of using his skin creams. Didn't really want to since they left Bo's skin smooth and supple, such an erotic contrast to Max's own work-roughened skin.

"That's good, then, right?" Max wanted to ask more, like if that included blood tests, because he really wanted that kind of commitment from his man. He wanted to give it, too, so much so that he was nearly vibrating with the need to ask.

"Yeah, it's great," Bo muttered. He leant back and looked up at Max, worry etched into his expression, deepening the fine lines at the outer corner of his eyes. "Are you going to want me to leave now?"

Max tamped down his irritation that Bo would think so little of him. One thing he'd become aware of since they'd made love the first time was that Bo, despite his swagger, suffered from a truckload of insecurity.

"Of course I want you here," Max soothed. "I'll always want you here."

Bo looked thunderstruck at the confession, his mouth flapping without making a sound. His eyes were welling with tears that he rapidly blinked away. The need to reassure him rode Max hard, and he wondered if he should alter his plans a bit, tell Bo how he felt before they sat down for their romantic dinner. Would it really matter if he said *I love you* before they ate? Would Bo throw his arms around him and admit that he loved Max as well, like Max knew he did?

Max was scared shitless to say those words, which was stupid. He knew he loved Bo, knew it was reciprocal. It was still scary since Max had never said those words to anyone else, ever.

"Do you mean that?" Bo's expression shifted from hopeful to fearful, repeating that pattern as he fidgeted in Max's arms.

"I do," Max promised. He felt the ball of nervous tension uncoil in his belly at the sweet smile that chased away everything except joy from Bo's face. Seeing Bo's eyes gleaming with happiness made the words come easy. "I love you, Bo."

Those words didn't light Bo up like Max had expected. Instead his lover shuddered in his arms then shoved Max back a step. "You don't! You can't, Max!"

Max frowned and struggled unsuccessfully to keep Bo in his arms. "I can and I do!"

Bo darted past him and ran into the kitchen. Max was practically right on his heels, which didn't work out so well when Bo came to a sudden stop. Max slammed into his back and cracked the bottom half of his face against the back of Bo's head. He managed to wrap his arms around Bo and twist around as they slammed into the floor. Max's breath spewed from his lungs as his back hit the hardwood floor, followed immediately by Bo's weight coming down on his chest. He rolled them to their sides, gasping for air, as he locked his squirming lover in his arms.

"Ain't letting you run off, Bo," Max murmured against the man's ear. "You're going to have to accept that I love you, and I think you love me, too."

Bo whimpered and shook his head. "I do, Max," although he couldn't say the words just yet, "how could I not? But you can't love me! You haven't ever been with anyone else, this could just be an infatuation or —"

Max rolled Bo to his back and took his mouth in a kiss he had meant to be tender but was more than a little angry and possessive. When he ended the kiss, Bo looked blissed out, his full lips rosy and more plump than usual, his eyes filled with a dazed look.

"I told you I can, and that's all that matters." Max had to take another nip of those sweet lips. Bo moaned and bucked beneath him, stabbing at Max's taut stomach with his erection. "I don't know why you think you're unloveable, but that ain't the case."

Bo blinked furiously but it didn't help this time. Tears spilled, rolling from the corners of his eyes, over his temples and into his hair. "I want to believe you, I do, but you haven't had any other sexual experience except what we've done together."

Max pushed himself up on his elbows and glared. "So, what? You saying you won't believe I love you 'til I've gone out and fucked a few men? Or does it need to be more?"

Bo nearly headbutted Max in his attempt to sit up. "No! That isn't what I meant! Just...maybe you should explore your options."

"I don't have any other options," Max snapped, his patience evaporated. "I don't *want* any other options!"

"You don't know that!"

Max stood up, grabbing one of Bo's wrists as he did so. "Yes, I do know that! I never wanted anyone before you, Bo, and I don't want anyone else now!"

Bo's expression showed his disbelief.

"I'm going to get this through to you one way or another," Max snapped. "I hope to hell dinner is still good when I'm done with you." Max jerked on Bo's arm and had the man over his shoulder before Bo could protest. "Blow out the candle." Max slapped Bo on the ass and turned around so Bo was facing the candle. He heard and felt the expulsion of breath as Bo blew the flickering flame out. "All right then, let's go."

He ignored Bo's protests that Max couldn't really love him, his wiggling, everything but his need to make Bo believe him. He opened the door to their room and within three steps, he was dropping Bo onto the surface of their bed. Max pointed a finger at him and used his sternest voice.

"You're going to tell me what the problem is, and you're going to do it now." Max tumbled onto the bed and pulled Bo against his side. "You are going to understand that I love you and don't want anybody else, ever."

Bo sniffled and shrugged his shoulders. "I think you believe it, at least."

That wasn't going to do at all. It would take some convincing, but Max was going to prove to Bo that he was worth being loved, and that Max was just the man to do it.

Chapter Thirteen

Bo was torn. He thought he should keep some space between them, but he wanted to snuggle in close and soak up the comfort that seemed to roll off Max in waves — except then he'd be more likely to babble. There was nothing like feeling safe to loosen Bo's tongue, as he'd found out since falling for Max. If he was going to have to talk, though, he'd rather stick to the bare boned facts. Bo started to roll away, intent on sitting up and putting a little distance between them. Max made a noise that sounded like a snarl and pulled Bo back to his side, one rough hand carefully pressing Bo's head until he rested it on Max's chest.

"Want you right here," Max said firmly even as his hands stroked gently over Bo's back. "You don't realise I got you figured out. You think scooting away a bit's going to give you some emotional distance, but I want everything, Bo. Bad and good. If you really want me to let you go, though, I will."

Bo considered his options, which were to talk, or not, move away or stay. He slid his hand down the ridged plane of Max's shirt-covered abdomen, wishing the material would magically vanish. His fingers teased at the waistband of Max's jeans then dipped beneath it and the elastic of the boxers. Before he could plunge his hand down further to grasp Max's cock, his wrist was caught in a strong grasp.

"That ain't going to work this time," Max told him, sounding more amused than irritated. "I went forty-three years without anyone else touching me, I can do without as long as it takes to get you to talk to me."

Bo yanked his wrist out of Max's hold and pushed himself up so he could glare down at his lover. "You're telling me you won't put out until I talk? What the hell?" His stomach clenched then did a little fear inspired dip. "You don't want me like I want you." The realisation hurt, like someone poured acid on every one of his nerve endings.

Max sat up and wrapped his arms around Bo. He flopped back and took Bo with him, laying them both out on the bed. "I *do* want you, Bo, more than you could ever know, which is *why* I want you to tell me what your reasoning is for thinking I don't know who or what I want." Max cupped Bo's jaw and tipped his head up, forcing Bo to meet his worried gaze. "I want to know why you think you don't deserve to be loved. I want the doubts and fears, not just the laughter and joy. I told you, Bo — the good *and* the bad. Do you want any less from me?"

"Well, when you say it like that..." Damn man would have to turn it right around on him, wouldn't he? But maybe that's exactly what Bo needed, someone who wouldn't be swayed by the promise of a tight ass, who cared enough about Bo, the person, to push aside Bo's attempts at deflection. Maybe Max wasn't rejecting him, but offering him everything, if Bo would only take the chance. Besides, what did he have to lose? He already loved Max insanely, and he trusted Max not to hurt him. Which meant the only reason Bo was clinging to his silence was pride. "Shit. I can be such an ass."

Max's chuckle filled Bo with reassuring warmth. "You ain't an ass, honey, just someone who's been hurt, like most of us have. You just have to know when to let go of the hurt. You're safe with me, Bo. I won't turn away from you for anything."

It was the calm, steady love lacing Max's voice and flickering in his nut-brown eyes that convinced Bo. That, and the endearment. It wasn't the first time he'd been called 'honey', but it was the first time anyone had ever said it with such tenderness. Still, his cheeks started burning, a heat which spread all the way down to his chest.

"It's stupid," Bo muttered. Plenty of people had faced a hell of a lot worse than him and come out just fine.

"Nothing that makes you hurt is stupid," Max said. Bo felt the barest brush of lips against his temple. He listened to the steady thrumming of Max's heart, the muted whoosh of his lover's breaths, until his lungs worked in synch with Max's.

Closing his eyes, Bo exhaled and forced himself to speak. "I guess...maybe it all started with my momma. Don't know who my daddy was, and from all the talk in the family, she probably didn't, either. She was a partier, and her parents had washed their hands of her years before I was born. The only things I know about her came from them, along with the story of how I ended up being abandoned. I wasn't even a year old when she went off to some party and left me alone in the crib. Left a few bottles of juice, and that was all. Didn't tell no one, didn't ask anyone to check on me—nothing. The cops said it was probably a couple of days I was alone until one of the neighbours in the next apartment called in because they'd heard me screaming, then…not. Someone noticed no one had come and gone from the apartment. If they hadn't called, I'd have been dead before morning."

"Bo, Jesus…" Max's arms tightened around Bo, nearly squeezing the breath out of him. "I'm so sorry, honey. Some people shouldn't ever be parents. Please tell me the police put her ass in jail."

Bo shook his head and bit back the hysterical laugh that threatened to break free. "Nope. No one knows what happened to her. She vanished. I used to think maybe she meant to come back for me, but her folks—my grandparents—told me she'd packed up all her shit when she left, so she meant for me to die. I don't know why she—" *Why she hated me.*

"She was a waste of a human being," Max rasped, his voice thick and gravelly. "She didn't deserve you, but I thank God that she had you, and if I can find those neighbours, I'll go thank them, drop right down on my knees and worship at their feet for saving you." A series of kisses landed on Bo's forehead and cheek. "You know that was her being a mess, it wasn't your fault?"

"Yeah, I know that up here"—Bo tapped at his head—"but it won't sink in, not when my first memories are of my grandparents telling me what a burden I was, and how they shouldn't have to raise a bastard like me." Bo ignored Max's curses and continued. "They died when I was six, a house fire when I'd been sent to stay with one of my aunts for the weekend. Grandpa was a heavy smoker, and you know the rest of that story. Falling asleep with a lit cigarette doesn't turn out well for anyone. After that, I was passed around to whatever relative would put up with me for a while. Not a one of them wanted me, but they were all pretty image-conscious and didn't want to appear to be the heartless people they were, you know. So in public they tolerated me, but in private..." Bo could still hear the hateful comments, the crushing words that destroyed a lonely little boy's hope for love. "In private, they let me know just how much they didn't want me. Even had a couple of them tell me I should have died when my momma ran off."

Max rumbled and Bo could feel the man's muscles tensing, could almost scent his anger. Instead of a trite line, though, Max merely said, "I'm sorry, honey. You know I mean it, but you need to tell me the rest."

Bo opened his eyes and glanced up at Max, who was looking at him with that shining burst of love in his dark eyes. "How did you know there's more to it than the poor, unloved orphan story?"

Max's lips tipped up in the barest of grins. "'Like I said, I *know* you. I don't know your past, but you, well, sometimes it's like you're so deep under my skin I can hear your thoughts, you know?"

Bo blinked. "That's actually kind of creepy, Max." Or kind of sweet.

"Nah." Max shrugged his shoulders, jostling Bo. "Ain't creepy, just means I pay attention to you, and not only when we're making love. It means I see *you*, not that flirty dude you show everyone else."

"I flirt with you, too," Bo pointed out, but he couldn't look into Max's eyes any longer, not when he knew Max could read everything Bo felt.

"Sure you do, but it ain't an act when you do it with me, not like it is with Rory or Chance."

"No, it isn't," Bo agreed. "I'm not teasing with you. I'm really offering."

Max's fingers traced over Bo's jaw, then hooked under his chin, tipping his head up. Bo opened his eyes and found himself pinned by Max's penetrating stare. "And did anyone else ever think it was an offer when it wasn't?"

Bo's mouth dropped open as he shivered. "How do you *do* that? That's just fucking scary!"

"Bo..." Max sighed as Bo continued to look at him, waiting for an explanation. "It's just from years of watching people, okay? Trying to figure out why people do what they do. It was easier than trying to figure out my own mess."

Max had told Bo about his own childhood, which was as fucked up as Bo's in its own way. Bo wouldn't have wanted to deal with it, either—much like he hadn't dealt with his own past. But Max was a stronger man than he ever would be.

He realised Max was waiting for an answer. Bo looked away and nodded once, a sharp, jerky movement that was more like a muscle spasm in his neck than an admission. "Yeah. First time was when I was fourteen and just figured out I found boys attractive instead of girls. Saw this one guy at the convenience store by where I was living, and he was...he was big, all masculine and hard and everything I wasn't. Caught him looking at me and thought I'd be cute, wink a time or two, shake my ass when I walked off. Didn't know he was following me. I didn't get more than a block before he pulled over and offered me a ride. I was a dumb kid, and he...he told me I wanted it, that I looked like I wanted it, so he...he did—"

"Bo," Max whispered, trying to tug him up higher.

Bo ignored him. "He kept me for hours, made sure I knew everything that could go on between two guys. I couldn't tell anyone, either, once he showed me his badge. No one would take my word over a cop's, and my family would have disowned me. Couldn't have a fag in the family, you know. They would have said it was my fault, and it was, since I'd looked at him like that and—"

"Bo!" Max thundered, snapping Bo back to the present, tearing him out of memories that still made his body tremble with remembered pain. "It wasn't your fault, you *know* that! You were just a kid, and he was someone who abused you and the trust his position implied."

"I know," Bo murmured, "but it happened more than once—not with him, never saw him again. I just stepped right into the pattern of being a victim, setting myself up to be one. Then one day I realised I was going to get myself killed like that, and as much as I didn't like myself, I did like living. I started flirting and offering, and *controlling* what happened."

"No, you were still a victim," Max argued. "You just switched it up to where you could tell yourself you weren't, that you were putting out willingly, but you were doing it to keep from being...being hurt again. If you gave it away, they couldn't take it, could they? And you never thought you deserved any better because, what? You thought you were dirty, maybe?"

Bo felt scraped raw from the inside out. Max had it figured out, mostly. "Damaged," Bo corrected. "Unlovable. Undeserving. Good for nothing but a place for some guy to—"

"Bullshit!" Max rolled them over, pinning Bo with his weight. He tilted up Bo's chin. Bo tried not to look at Max, tried to keep from raising his eyes, but he couldn't resist, not when he knew Max would wait with all the patience Bo'd never had. He managed to look at Max through nearly-closed lids. "All those people, none of them saw you, honey. Not a one of them bothered to look. Not when you were a little boy, aching to belong, to be loved, not when you were a confused teenager who needed support, not when you were a grown man who still had those two wounded versions of himself as a kid locked inside. Instead, you were hurt, and maybe you let yourself be used later on, because you didn't know any other way, but that don't mean you deserved any of it, Bo."

Bo wanted to believe Max, but he didn't know how. He started to shake his head only to remember that Max still cupped his chin. Max's eyes were welling with the threat of tears, the tip of his nose red, but he looked at Bo with so much love that Bo didn't know how to handle it. He began to shake, as if his body wanted to turn inside out, deep, gut-wrenching shudders that caused his muscles to cramp and his lungs to squeeze out each breath in a rasping pant. He dimly realised that his face was wet, that even now tears were running from the outer edges of his eyes, down to his temples and into his hair.

Max rolled them again until Max was on his back and Bo was laying on him. Bo buried his head against Max's neck, gritting his teeth through the racking spasms that shook him. He slowly became aware of Max's murmured words of love in his ear, of Max's hands caressing him, his strong arms holding Bo.

"I love you, honey," Max uttered over and over as Bo struggled to get himself together, yet every time Max said those words, Bo's heart ached with his desire to believe them.

"How can you?" Bo finally asked when he could unclench his jaw. He felt shredded, utterly demolished and shattered.

"How can I not?" Max countered. "I've waited my whole life just for you, Bo, forty-three years, just for you.

You're the only person who's ever made me want anything, and I will love you every minute of this lifetime and every minute after it, too."

Some of the shards started mending themselves back together with Max's declaration. Slowly, the pain began to ebb, not leaving, but simmering to a bearable throb. Bo studied Max intently, seeing everything he'd ever wanted, everything he'd ever needed there in Max's dark eyes—if he could only just believe.

"You're everything I want," Max rasped. "More than I deserve, but I'm keeping you. You say I'm a good man, right?"

"The best," Bo agreed.

"Then trust me to love you," Max urged. "Trust me to know that you deserve it, and maybe you'll see that you really do. Please, honey, let me."

Bo couldn't deny Max anything, not when Bo loved the man with an intensity that rocked him to his very soul. "I will," he promised, feeling a little bit more of the pain slide away. "I do." *And I love you so much, you wonderful, stubborn, sexy man.* And Bo would tell him that, just as soon as he could say it without trembling in fear. He knew in his heart Max wouldn't reject him, now he just had to get the message through to his brain.

Chapter Fourteen

Bo was waiting for him on the porch as had become his habit the last several days. Seeing his lover sitting there chased the tired right out of Max's body, and his cock was well on its way to being erect before he even made it up the stairs. Usually Bo greeted him with a heart-melting smile, but this evening Bo sat stiffly in the chair, nibbling on his lower lip. His pensive expression had Max rethinking his plans to drag the man inside and show Bo just how much he'd missed him since this morning.

"Something on your mind?" Max asked as he pulled a chair close to Bo's and sat down. Bo blinked several times and nodded.

"Yeah, yeah, I..." Bo swallowed noisily. He looked nervous, and worse, *scared*. Max didn't like that at all. He reached for Bo's hand and felt a bolt of panic when he realised Bo's hand was shaking.

"What's wrong, honey?" Max hoped Bo wasn't giving up. He knew his lover was trying to believe Max loved him, would *always* love him, but Bo was battling a lifetime of neglect and feelings of unworthiness. Not an insurmountable task, but damned close maybe. Max cupped Bo's cheek and kissed him, a languorous, thorough kiss that left them both breathless. The fear was gone from Bo's eyes, replaced by the same burning need that had simmered in Max's veins all day. But as much as he wanted to make love to Bo, it would have to wait. Too many people had been willing to plunder Bo's body without giving a damn about his heart. Max wasn't such a fool. "Tell me what's on your mind."

Bo looked confused for a moment then he shook his head, as if to bring his mind back to order. "You know I had another nightmare last night."

Max was well aware. Bo had woken him with whimpers that turned into pleas then escalated into cries for help before Max had finally managed to pull his lover from whatever hellish nightmare he'd had.

"Yeah, but you fell asleep again almost immediately." And Max hadn't been able to ask about the dream, although it sounded like the others, which Bo had told him were vivid nightmares about the assault several weeks ago.

Bo nodded as if he'd read Max's thoughts. "Yeah, it's the same one I keep having. I thought, maybe, if you're up to it, we could…" Bo shuddered and continued. "The three of us, you, me, and Annabelle, we could maybe go to The Xxchange tonight. Replace the bad memory of a club with a good one, you know?"

Max was ninety-nine-point-nine percent sure he'd rather be shot than go out to some club like The Xxchange, but he'd do damn near anything for Bo. But he did wonder. "That the only reason you want to go? You were so worried I only wanted you because I hadn't ever had anyone else."

Bo blushed and glanced at his feet. "I'm trying, Max, you have to know that. But it wouldn't hurt if you danced with a few guys, see if you felt anything—"

Max bit back a groan. "Bo, I can't do that. I can't just...just let some guy grope me." The idea alone filled him with terror. Letting some stranger touch him, flirt with him, it made those walls that Bo had torn down slam right back up. Bo was the only one he ever wanted to touch him like that. Which was why, he realised, it might be a good idea after all. If Bo saw Max cringe every time a guy approached him—which probably wouldn't happen at all. Max knew he was a worn old cowboy, nothing special to look at.

"Please, Max." Bo's earnest expression was definitely tipping Max towards agreeing, but Bo's next words clinched it. "And maybe if we go to the club, even though it isn't the same one where I was attacked, maybe going will help me with the nightmares. You know, having a good time could hopefully replace the bad memories. I'm scared to go, but I think I need to."

Max mulled it over for less than a minute. "Yeah, okay, but here's the rules. I don't have to dance with anyone else. Why you'd want me to I don't understand,"— *mostly*—"because I sure as hell don't want to see you in some other guy's arms."

Bo looked like he wanted to argue, but he nodded with almost no hesitation.

"And I don't want any of this jealous stuff," Max emphasised. "If someone's looking at you or me, ain't either of us going to act on it, so there's no reason for hurt feelings. We can't help what other people do, but we can sure be responsible for what we do."

"Okay," Bo agreed softly. "But if you *do* see someone you want—"

"I won't," Max said, cutting Bo off briskly. "You sure you want Annabelle to come with us?" Did Bo think Max was going to run off with some other man and leave him alone at The Xxchange? Max was afraid to ask, because if Bo said yes, Max might just lose his temper and say something he'd regret. He was doing his best, but Bo's doubts cut him sometimes, deep enough that Max wondered how there weren't any scars.

Bo shifted in his chair until he was twisted around fully facing Max. "I wanted her to come for a couple of reasons. First, she's become one of my closest friends." Max could see that. He thought the same of Annabelle as well. "Second, I just…I think I'd feel safer, the more of us there are, you know? That's not an insult to you, just the whole 'safety in numbers' thing. I want this trip to a club to be as different from the last as possible."

Max would see to it that it was. "Me, too. Let's go see if Annabelle's up for a night out."

* * * *

"You doing all right?"

Bo tried not to roll his eyes at Annabelle. He wasn't very successful. "You and Max have asked me that at least half a dozen times, and we haven't even walked in the door!"

Annabelle rolled her eyes back, and did it much more dramatically. Bo was going to have to get some pointers from this chick. "So what if we have? It just means we love you, and you *didn't* answer my question."

A warm, fuzzy feeling at Annabelle's declaration chased off Bo's jangling nerves. "I'm fine, really, now can we have some fun?"

"That's the plan," Max said, apparently willing to speak since Bo's snark encounter with Annabelle had passed. Bo took Annabelle's hand in his left one and wound his right arm around his lover's hips. Max put his arm on Bo's shoulders, his fingertips teasing over Bo's biceps. Annabelle pulled open the door to The Xxchange, grinning as eardrum-splitting…well, Bo wouldn't call it music, exactly. It was loud, and there was some kind of instruments involved, and someone was screeching—

"Oh!" Annabelle squealed and clapped her hands. "Soluble Mass Exodus is playing! I *love* Soluble Mass Exodus! Come on!"

Max looked as stunned by Annabelle's behaviour as Bo felt. They entered the club behind her, and Max went from stunned to outright shocked, if Bo was reading his expression right, and he thought he was. He glanced in the direction Max was staring. Yup, it was definitely the kind of club Bo used to hang out in. There were three men not ten feet away, one man was kneeling, his head bobbing rhythmically, his right arm jerking his own cock. The guy getting blown wasn't good for much of anything just then, moaning and thrashing his head, his hips stuttering. The third man was doing his very best to rub off on the second man's hip. All in all, a scene Bo had not only viewed several times, but also participated in.

Bo looked away from the free porn—he'd seen better, and he had someone more interesting and sexy to look at now anyway. Max didn't look turned on by the display at all. Both his expression and his cock showed disinterest in the trio. Max shook his head and turned to Bo.

"Are you sure this is where you want to be tonight?" Max tipped his thumb at the now cummy three men. "'Cause I got to tell you, that don't do a thing for me. We got what, three feet in the door and I done seen more mens' cocks than I ever have in my life, and a live sex show. I am not impressed. I told you, you're the only person that turns me on, honey."

Bo opened his mouth to respond only to be cut off.

"Oh, God, how could you not think that was hot?" Annabelle fanned her flushed cheeks. "I mean, granted, that guy kneeling is kinda not all that, and the guy he was blowing has a really small dick, but—"

"Jesus, Annabelle!" Max grabbed her arm and jerked her behind his back. The look he shot Bo was filled with more than a little guilt. Bo felt bad for forgetting she was with them for a few minutes, but as for what she'd seen… Annabelle was an adult, she'd obviously enjoyed it. No reason to feel guilty for that in his book, though he knew he was going to have a hard time convincing Max to agree.

Annabelle snatched her arm back and glared at Max for a moment. Her expression softened suddenly, her lips tipping up in a slight smile. She patted Max's shoulder and gave him a quick kiss on the cheek, which caused a pretty red tint to spread up from Max's neck to his forehead.

"Max, you're the one who isn't used to this stuff. I've seen it before." Annabelle patted his shoulder once more then walked right past him into the heart of the club. She stopped and turned towards them, crooking a finger.

"I think she's not quite the vestal virgin you thought she was," Bo said next to Max's ear. "And you may be ready to go, and I might be too, but she isn't, and I don't think we're going to get her out of here any time soon."

"But—" Max stopped and straightened his shoulders as he stared at Annabelle. "I thought you said this was a gay club?" Bo's hand was taken and he was half-dragged towards Annabelle.

"It is. I mean, there's lesbians, too, and some bi's—oh." And there were several of both, Bo figured, checking Annabelle out thoroughly. "Let's get a table." Bo hooked his arm through Annabelle's and the three of them began working through gyrating bodies towards the bar and tables. Max swore soundly on more than one occasion, and pried off a determined dark-haired little twink—cute boy, tenacious, though.

Bo ended up leaning over and threatening to thrash the kid, who then suggested a threesome. He followed them to the table. Max looked like he was ready to strangle the twink with his long black hair.

"Look," the kid pleaded. "I'm open to a threesome, I just can't, uh, she'd have to be in the other room or something."

Annabelle sidled up to the poor pretty young thing and licked her lips as she dragged her gaze over him. Her method of getting rid of him worked better than Bo's or Max's.

"Son of a bitch grabbed my dick," Max snarled, "and my ass, and he wasn't the only one. I'm almost scared to try to leave. You get groped? Is that normal for a place... Guess it is for clubs like this, huh?"

Bo grinned at Max's obvious discomfort. Sweet man, putting himself in what had to be his version of hell just to make Bo feel secure. "There's nice clubs, too. This is just a meat market." Bo glanced around then watched as Annabelle tried to flag down a server. He couldn't quite bring himself to look at Max as he confessed, "You do know places like this were my usual hangouts, right? That what you've seen, I've probably done." *A lot.*

Max pulled Bo onto his lap. He cupped Bo's jaw and stroked his fingers over Bo's cheek. "I don't care what you *did*, Bo, I only care what you *do*."

The sincerity and love in Max's dark eyes and in his voice seeped into Bo, wrapping around his heart, shattering his fears, chipping at his doubts. When Max looked at him like that, Bo could believe he deserved to be loved, and maybe, when he forgot it at times, he'd be able to remember this moment to help him feel worthy of Max.

And hadn't Max ignored every other man here, unless he was snarling at them? The erection bumping at Bo's butt was the first one Max had got since they entered this place.

"What more do you need, honey? Tell me, I'll do it."

What more *did* he need? Coming to this club tonight had proven several things to Bo. The first and most important he'd already noted. Max wasn't interested in anyone else. Second, Bo was able to walk into the place, so much like the club he'd been to in San Antonio, and not feel more than a small fissure of fear, at least not with Max and Annabelle at his sides. And finally, tonight had helped to bury one of Bo's secret concerns — that he'd be tempted by the familiar environment and feel the urge to fall back into the role he used to play. Max wasn't the only one who hadn't noticed any other man.

"I want you to take me home and make love to me," Bo whispered in Max's ear, nibbling on the sweet skin. Max shuddered beneath him as Bo licked and sucked on the sensitive spot right beneath his lobe. Strong arms wrapped around him, pulling him closer. Max's lips brushed over Bo's cheek, his jaw, placing biting kisses up to his ear. His body tensed as Max whispered, "How 'bout *you* make love to *me*?"

"Oh, God," Bo whimpered. He ground his ass against Max's hard length as he clutched at Max's shoulders. "Yes, please!" Bo hadn't got to top often and was pretty much fine with that, but he wanted to feel Max's body clamping down on him more than he wanted to live another day. "Can we go home now?"

Max chuckled and nipped at his neck. "Thought you'd never ask."

"I'm not going to get to finish my drink, am I?" Annabelle asked, sounding amused and grinning from ear to ear.

"'Fraid not," Max agreed. "Let's go home."

Chapter Fifteen

The drive back to the ranch had been quiet, the tension in the cab of the truck palpable and thicker than wet cement. Max had been having second, third, and fourth thoughts about his words to Bo. He hadn't even thought before he said it, just opened his mouth and out tumbled the desire he'd kept tucked away. Fear of the unknown had bound Max's curiosity, but the need to share every part of himself with Bo unlocked Max's desires and momentarily demolished his fears. By the time they pulled into the drive, Max was wound up tight and afraid he wouldn't be able to go through with it. Despite the fact Bo obviously loved having Max's cock in his ass, Max couldn't see how *he* was going to be able to relax enough to enjoy Bo doing him.

On the other hand, he really, really wanted to know what it'd feel like to have Bo deep inside him. More than that, he wanted to do this for Bo, offer up his love and trust by offering his body. Bo would see it for the gift and commitment it was, he'd be careful, loving, patient—but Max was still scared spitless.

"We don't have to," Bo murmured. Max looked up and realised he'd stopped at the foot of the porch steps. His lover stood on the porch, watching him. Max couldn't make out Bo's features in the starless night, but he knew the understanding lacing Bo's voice would be in the man's expression as well. Max shrugged his shoulders, trying to roll away some of his anxiety.

"I want to, just nervous," he confessed. "I don't know if I can…if I'll like it like you do, you know?"

Bo came down the steps and slid his arms around Max's waist. He put his head on Max's shoulder and burrowed his lips and nose against Max's neck, licking and sucking until a different kind of tension coiled in Max. "We don't have to," Bo repeated. "But if you want to try, I promise I'll stop the second you tell me to if you hate it."

The warm breath slicking over wet skin caused Max to shiver as he clutched at Bo's chest. "Okay," Max rasped, unable to say anything more when his whole body was vibrating with desire. Having Bo pressed up against him, that denim-clad cock rubbing against his own, was firing up every one of Max's fantasies.

Bo's hands drifted down to Max's ass and squeezed his cheeks. "Come on, then," he said with a pat to Max's butt. "Maybe Annabelle's already asleep. She practically ran inside and went straight to her room."

Max nodded and let Bo lead him into the bunkhouse.

"Do you want something to drink first?" Bo asked. "Some water, or maybe something stronger? A shot or two of whisky might help you relax."

Now that they were inside, Max had no trouble making out the concern in Bo's expression. He shook his head and tipped his chin towards their room. "I don't want any alcohol. Don't want it to interfere with what I'm feeling, you know? I can trust you to make sure I'm ready."

A soft, loving look came over Bo. "Yes, you can. I haven't topped often, but I know what feels good, and what feels great, from the bottom." Bo clasped Max's hand tightly. They walked to their room together, shoulders bumping with each step they took. Max was trying to breathe normally as his fear gave way to anticipation.

Once inside the room, Bo locked the door. They tugged off their boots then faced each other. Max hesitated to make the first move, unsure in this situation and feeling vulnerable. Bo stroked Max's cheek tenderly then cupped the back of Max's neck. Max parted his lips under Bo's, moaning as his lover kissed him. The gentle swipe of Bo's tongue became more forceful as they grappled at each other's clothes.

Their fingers bumped and tangled at Max's belt until Bo growled into the kiss, sending a shiver through Max. His hands dropped to his sides as he let Bo have his way. It was surprisingly erotic to hand Bo the lead, and Max felt tingles in places he hadn't ever thought to. As Bo shoved Max's pants and boxers down, his hand trailed over Max's hips. The tips of his fingers brushed over the sides of Max's ass, and he gasped as his hole clenched and fluttered. Relaxing might not be the problem he'd thought it would be.

Bo chuckled and unbuttoned Max's shirt as he nibbled along his jaw. Once Max was divested of his clothes, Bo nudged him backwards, still nibbling and sucking on Max's stubbled skin. The backs of Max's legs hit the mattress then he was tumbling onto the bed. He caught himself on his elbows and looked up at Bo. The confidence and desire he saw in his lover's eyes firmed Max's dick until it was achingly hard. Bo slid his gaze over Max's shaft and Max felt it like a caress. Pre-cum beaded at the tip, and Bo's smile faded as he licked his lips. He trailed a finger over the weeping slit and Max hissed as his balls pulled tight.

"I do love you," Bo said when he finally looked away from Max's cock. Before Max could reply, Bo dropped to his knees between Max's thighs. He tugged off Max's socks, which he hadn't even realised he was wearing any more, and shoved Max's legs further apart. Max opened his mouth to tell Bo he loved him, too, but Bo's head dipped and the feel of a wet tongue lapping at Max's balls turned his words into a loud moan.

Bo sucked a nut into his mouth as his hands slid under Max's ass, cupping his cheeks. Max panted and undulated as Bo worked both of Max's balls into his mouth, his tongue swirling and prodding the furry orbs until Max cried out, "Please, Bo! God! I need...I need...something!"

Bo released his balls, stood up, and quickly removed his clothes. "Put your feet on the bed." Bo lifted one of Max's legs, bending it at the knee as Max followed suit with the other. In no time Bo had him spread out, his heels pressing against his ass, and his ass almost hanging off the bed. Max felt wanton and embarrassed and so horny he thought he'd come if Bo even breathed on his dick.

Bo stood looking down at him, gripping the base of his cock, his hazel eyes burning a trail up Max's body. When he spoke, his voice was raw and low. "Max, could you do something for me?"

"Anything," Max answered, not having to give it a thought.

Bright spots sprouted on Bo's cheeks and his confident look wavered for a moment. He shrugged and straightened his shoulders and Max found his admiration for his lover increasing as he watched the man find the determination to ask for what he wanted. "You don't have to, but I'd love to see you play with your nipples while I suck your cock." Bo shuddered and closed his eyes. "That'd be so fucking hot, knowing you were getting off on your hands and my mouth working your body."

"Shit." Max's dick oozed pre-cum now. He wasn't sure he could touch himself like that and not blow his load all over the damn place, especially not while Bo was sucking him in, but he'd try. Instead of answering, Max brought his hands to his belly and trailed his fingers up from below his naval, over his ribs and up to his chest. By the time he brushed over his nipples, Bo was whimpering and dropping to his knees. Max did some whimpering of his own as he plucked at his nipples. The feel of Bo's tongue swiping at his balls, then lower still to the sensitive patch of skin under them changed Max's whimpers to moans. Bo suckled on that spot and Max had to grab his cock, pinching the base as hard as he could stand to keep from coming.

"Bo, please, I can't hold back much longer," Max pleaded.

"Then don't. I promise I'll get you hard again, work you right back up so you're ready for me."

Max wasn't so sure about that but Bo's mouth enveloping his shaft took the decision out of his hands. Bo sucked him all the way down until his lips nudged Max's hand. He released his cock and groaned as the final inch sank into Bo's mouth. A slick finger teased at Max's hole, adding a delicious pressure to that aching entry just as Bo swallowed around Max's dick. Max shouted as a wildfire roared through him. Bo's finger sank inside Max's ass and Max came in deep, wrenching spurts. Bo pulled back, swallowing Max's spunk as his finger pumped in and out of Max's hole.

Max yelped and his shoulders came up off the bed as Bo's finger brushed over his gland. "Ohmyfuckinggod! Bo!" Max had never felt anything like that before. It was as if every nerve ending was supersensitised and swelling under an onslaught of ecstasy. His cock hadn't even had the chance to fully soften, and as it slipped from Bo's mouth, Bo rubbed at that spot deep inside Max again. Max clutched at the blanket as his head spun and his eyes rolled back.

Max panted and moaned as Bo went back to suckling at his balls. His legs fell open wider, and soon the tender skin on the insides of his thighs was licked and sucked. Max's skin prickled and his thighs quivered as Bo sucked at one particularly sensitive spot. The scrape of teeth over it made Max's eyes cross. There'd likely be a bruise there tomorrow. Max hoped so; he liked the idea of Bo marking him somewhere only the two of them would know.

Bo purred and nuzzled Max's balls. "Love this, love the way you smell, the way you taste, the sounds you make, how your body responds just for me…"

Max's body was responding, all right. He felt flushed from head to toe and his skin tingled and prickled with goose bumps. That finger working in and out of his opening was making him feel heated from the inside out, and every time Bo brushed over his gland, Max's cock jerked and thumped his belly.

"Look at you, giving yourself to me so beautifully. Nobody's ever given me so much, Max, no one but you."

Bo's words were every bit as stimulating as his touch, and Max wanted to say something back, tell Bo how much he loved him, how he'd do anything for the man, but Max's tongue seemed thick, his mouth and throat dry as pleasure suffused his body. A bite to the underside of his thigh where ass and leg met had Max arching, fireworks exploding in his vision.

"Uuungh!" Blood rushed to Max's shaft, bringing him to full, aching hardness. There was a burning sensation as another finger was pushed into his hole. Before Max could focus on the burn, Bo found that magic spot again and all Max could do was pant and moan and shove his ass towards those fingers. Max lost himself in the sensation of being filled. He forgot to be scared, forgot about pride, instead thrusting and pleading for *moremoremorenow!*

Bo's fingers slid out of Max's ass and Max started to protest. "I've got you, baby," Bo murmured. "Need to get ready to take you."

Max craned his neck and watched as Bo plucked up a condom. He opened the package and sheathed his cock quickly then pumped his length a few times. Max snarled with impatience as Bo popped open the lube and poured a dollop into his hand. Bo gave him an amused, needy look. "Trust me, you'll be glad I spared a few seconds for the lube."

Max opened his mouth to argue the point then thought better of it. As aroused as he was, now Bo's fingers were out of him, Max could actually think. That wasn't necessarily a good thing, because while he agreed with Bo, he was now feeling a bit of apprehension. Bo's dick was a hell of a lot thicker and longer than two or three fingers. His worry must have been evident because Bo picked up on it immediately.

"It'll be fine, you'll see," Bo said. "Can you scoot to the middle of the bed? Or, it'd be easier for you if you lay on your stomach or –"

"I'll move," Max interrupted. Being on his stomach might be easier, but he wanted to be able to see Bo this first – and maybe only – time. He positioned himself in the centre of the bed. It was hard for Max to spread his legs, knowing what was about to happen, but the memory of Bo's fingers filling him and brushing over that spot was all the encouragement he needed. Max stuffed down his fear and spread his legs as wide as he could make himself.

Bo crawled onto the bed and sat on his heels between Max's thighs. He leant forward and grabbed a pillow. "Lift your hips." Max did and Bo slid the pillow underneath him. "Now, where were we? Oh yeah."

Bo sprawled on top of Max and sought his lips. Max opened for his lover, spearing his tongue into Bo's mouth as he grabbed a double handful of Bo's ass. Bo moaned and bit at Max's lips. He ground down and rubbed his sheathed dick alongside Max's. The feel of that thick length on his had Max's hole fluttering and he was ready to beg all over again.

"I know," Bo whispered against Max's lips. "Makes you ache so good, doesn't it?"

Max nodded and shifted his legs. "Please, Bo..."

Bo kissed him again, sweet and possessive, then rose and nudged Max's legs. He helped Max hook them over Bo's shoulders, then Bo was spreading his own legs and guiding his dick to Max's ass. The first press of Bo's fat crown against Max's opening had Max trying to clench his body shut even as he yearned to feel Bo take him. Bo murmured softly and stroked Max's thighs even as he forged forward. Bo's cockhead plunged into Max's opening, stretching the guardian muscle wide.

It burned all the way up Max's rectum and Max gasped, thinking maybe he couldn't do this after all. His muscles clenched before Max could stop them and Bo's cock slid in deeper, chasing away the first burst of pain and filling Max with a strange sensation of being filled near to bursting. It didn't hurt, exactly, and Max thought he might even come to like the feeling.

"You doing okay now?" Bo's worried voice had Max opening eyes he hadn't even been aware he'd closed.

Max put his hands on Bo's where they gripped his thighs. "Doesn't hurt much now, just feels...kinda weird. But not bad," he added to clarify.

Bo's smile said he understood perfectly. "It's fixing to go from not hurting much and weird to mind-blowing, I promise."

"I—fuck!" Max couldn't think any more, not with Bo steadily sliding in to the hilt. Before Max could even draw a breath, Bo shifted his hips and his cock rubbed up against Max's gland. Max wanted more of that ecstasy, more of his blood singing through his veins and his body flying with the feelings only Bo could give him. "Move! God, now, Bo!"

"Thought you'd never ask." Bo dropped his chin to his chest and began pumping into Max, slow, small movements at first that made Max want to snarl with frustration. Right before he was ready to snap, Bo started spearing hard and deep, his dick rubbing Max's gland with every inward thrust. Max thought he was going to lose his mind, the pleasure was so intense. He started jerking his hips up, trying to get more of his lover's length and get it in harder. Bo growled, the sound fuelling the tingling and tightening of Max's balls, and Bo began slamming into him, plundering Max so perfectly Max wanted to weep for joy.

Bo nudged Max's hand where it gripped his. "Gonna come, baby. Need to bring you with me—"

"Don't need a hand," Max gasped. His body was sparking with pleasure, his nipples peaked and burning, his cock throbbing. "Gonna—*gaawwwdd!*" Max howled as cum sprayed from his shaft. His vision dimmed as wet heat splattered onto his chest. Bo grunted and shoved his cock deep into Max's ass. He froze as he moaned. Even in the stunned throes of his climax, Max felt Bo's shaft swell and throb inside him. Bo shuddered and moaned again as he ground against Max's ass. Max shot more cum onto his stomach, gasping as each subsequent shot of semen spewed out.

"I don't want to pull out," Bo muttered, his voice rough.

"Don't want you to," Max muttered once he could speak.

"Got to, I think I probably poured a gallon of cum into the rubber." Bo stroked Max's thighs before carefully pulling out of Max's body. He removed the condom and tied it off then tossed it in the trash can beside the bed. "I'll get a washcloth."

Max shook his head and reached for his lover. Bo was trembling, shaking hard enough to make the bed vibrate. "Leave it, we can shower after we recover." He pulled Bo to him. Bo sighed and snuggled up to Max's side, swiping at some cum on Max's chest.

"You're a mess, and the sexiest thing I've ever seen," Bo teased, then spoke with an eloquence that belied his trembling body. "And I love you, Max, with everything I am and hope to be, and I know it's the truth when you say you love me, too. You've given me the strength to believe I deserve that."

"I couldn't ask for anything more," Max said as his heart swelled with love. "Except for this." He buried his fingers in Bo's hair and tipped his head up for a kiss. "Now I've got everything."

Chapter Sixteen

It was another unusually warm winter day and Max swiped at the sweat on his forehead then tucked the sopping bandana into his back pocket. He left the Stetson on a fence post as he crept towards the big house where Bo was ensconced in the small office Chance had set up for him. Once it'd been decided that Bo would be staying here, living with Max in the bunkhouse, Chance had offered Bo a job keeping the accounts for the ranch and putting to use the contacts Bo had accumulated when he'd been involved in the rodeo. Bo had a lot of contacts, but Max wasn't worried about it. Bo loved him, and that was all that mattered.

He toed off his boots and set them on the porch once he'd quietly cleared the steps. Hoping the screen door wouldn't squeak and give away his game, Max pulled the door open. He breathed a sigh of relief, grateful the oil he'd coated the hinges with had done its job. Padding through the house towards Bo's office, Max checked each room he passed. Rory and Chance were supposed to be out in the North pasture, but he wouldn't have put it past them to sneak home for some lunch time nooky. Of course, they were probably just going at it in the pasture, traumatising the cattle.

The door to Bo's office was open slightly, enough that Max could see a strip of blond hair streaked with grey and the sharp edge of a cheekbone. He heard Bo's muttered curse and what sounded like something small striking the wooden desktop.

"Damn it, how the fuck did I do that?"

Max grinned and pressed one hand to the door, nudging it open. Bo sat at the desk, his normally smooth brow wrinkled as he glared down at a paper in his hand.

"You having a bad day?" Max asked, delighted when Bo jumped and yelped.

Bo dropped the paper and pointed at him, his eyes narrowing even as his full lips twitched. "You shit! You nearly gave me a heart attack!"

Max chuckled and stepped into the room, enjoying the heat that flared in those hazel eyes when he closed the door and locked it. "I promise, that wasn't my intention."

Bo leant back in his chair and rubbed his chest with one hand. The other dropped below the desk top to rub at something else. Max's mouth watered as he took a few steps forward, gaze locked on the sight of Bo rubbing the bulge at his groin.

"And what was your intention?" Bo asked, his voice silky and warm, slicking over Max's cock and bringing him to achingly erect.

"I thought you might need a break," Max said, still watching that hand. He set his own to unbuttoning his shirt and jeans. "Looks like I was right. That hard on you got can't be comfortable."

Bo snorted and unfastened his jeans, his cock bobbing out proof that he had foregone his briefs. "It isn't, and it's taking away the blood from up here." Bo tapped his head. "No wonder I keep making stupid-ass mistakes."

"No wonder." Max shucked out of his clothes and strode over to his lover. He tapped the insides of Bo's thighs, encouraging him to spread his lean legs wider. Bo huffed and obediently did so. Max knelt between Bo's knees then reached for Bo's wrists. "Up, stand up."

Bo arched a brow but once again did as ordered. He started to lower his jeans more but Max stopped him. As much as he needed to taste Bo, he couldn't wait for the man to strip any further.

Bo stroked his fingers through Max's hair. He fisted his hands and pulled until Max was forced to look up at him instead of at the thickly veined dick bobbing in front of his face. "You in a hurry?"

"Yep." Admitting so wasn't a problem, and Bo's slit was already oozing pre-cum. Max wasn't the only one who was eager. Max stared up into his lover's eyes and gave him a wicked smile. "We only have an hour, and I want to bend you over the desk and bury my dick in that sweet ass, too." Saying it was nearly enough to make him come. Max pressed the heel of one hand to his engorged shaft and fondled Bo's rapidly drawing up balls with the other. Despite having balls of his own, those things just fascinated him. Or Bo's did, anyway. The texture of the wrinkled skin, the fuzz coating them, the way they did that—pulling up snug into hard nuts, Max loved playing with them, that was all there was to it. He scraped a nail over the tight sac and grinned when Bo moaned.

"Sounds perfect," Bo rasped, his voice high and shaky. "Could you get on with it?"

"I could if you'd quit trying to pull my hair out."

Bo grumbled but loosened his hold and Max dove for his lover's balls, drawing in a deep breath. The musky scent excited him unbearably and he lapped and nipped at the drawn up balls, one hand fisting the base of Bo's cock while the other clutched a firm ass cheek. He wiggled his fingers deeper into Bo's crack until his fingers brushed over Bo's hole. The shudder that rocked the man threatened to topple him so Max grudgingly left off teasing Bo's balls and pucker, guiding him instead to lean back against the desk.

"Better hold on now," Max warned then sealed his mouth around Bo's crown and sucked, hard. He delved the tip of his tongue into the slit and Bo cried out, his fingers once again fisting in Max's hair, pulling painfully. Max ignored it, increasing the suction until he'd milked all the pre-cum he could from Bo's dick. He backed off to swirl his tongue around the rim, teasing at the sensitive bundle of nerves on the underside. Bo's steady stream of curses and the shout he gave when Max swooped and suddenly engulfed his whole rod suffused Max with a rush of love and wonder. He hadn't ever thought to have this, to love and be loved in returned. That he did never failed to surprise and delight him, and he was determined to make sure Bo knew how much he was loved.

Swallowing around the swollen crown in his throat was a new trick he'd learned, and one that never failed to drive Bo over the edge. Bo howled and curled over him, pressing Max's brow against his thatch of pubic hair. As he pulled back to catch Bo's release on his tongue, Max kind of wished he'd had more restraint and had held off, sucked Bo's cock longer because he dearly loved doing this. But he wanted to feel Bo's tight ass clenching around his dick, soon. The feeling of those inner muscles massaging his length was exquisite. Max would never get enough.

"Shit, Max, that was…" Bo sighed and slowly untangled his fingers, rubbing Max's sore scalp. "You're really, really good at that," he purred as he unfolded himself until he was once more leaning against the desk.

Max lapped at the remaining cum leaking from Bo's slit before looking up into blue eyes shining bright with all the love Max had once thought he'd never have. "Only for you," Max promised, smiling at the way Bo seemed to melt at the words. "Only for you."

Chapter Seventeen

The bunkhouse felt empty with everybody gone. It wasn't often Bo found himself alone there anymore, and even though it was strange, he was glad. Tomorrow was Valentine's Day and he had plans for Maxie and himself. Ones they'd both enjoy.

He was also nervous as hell. This was the first year he'd ever had someone to spend February fourteenth with — in a relationship kind of way. He'd had more than his share of one-night stands on past Valentine's, other lonely men who didn't have anyone important to be with. Or maybe those guys had just been horny; there'd been plenty of times when that had been the case for Bo.

Now, however, he had one very special man to spend that holiday with, and Bo was scared he'd screw it all up. After all, what did he really know about Valentine's Day? Not a damn thing except for what he saw on TV and in the stores. Flowers, chocolates, and a card, those seemed to be the standard gifts, so Bo had got those after looking online for ideas had only netted him a boner and some rather surprisingly naughty gift suggestions. As much as he'd like to see Max bent over with a fat red plug topped with a heart handle poking out his ass, Bo didn't think his partner would be quite as turned on. Max was a wild man in bed — or wherever they decided to make love — but he was still a bit skittish when it came to using toys. Bo had only got him to use a dildo on him in the past month. Although, the man *really* liked watching that thing stretching and filling Bo's hole.

Bo liked it, too, and he'd like to use it on Max one day soon. He figured that was a possibility, what with the way Max seemed so…enthusiastic about using the dildo on him. The first time Max had turned beet red, but once Bo had moaned that flush had turned into one of arousal and Max had forgotten all about being embarrassed.

Jesus, it was making Bo hard just thinking about it! The phone rang and startled Bo enough that his erection withered. He got up off the couch and found the handset on the kitchen table. He didn't recognise the number, but the San Antonio area code made his heart slam into his ribs. No one from San Antonio called him. The last time had been the hospital trying to clear up a billing issue Bo had disputed. And before that it'd been the detective.

Bo answered the phone, fear and hope tangling into a ball in his belly. He greeted the caller then sat at the kitchen table when his knees threatened to give out. After grunting through most of the call, he managed some semblance of a polite goodbye then hung up and cradled his head in his hands and tried not to fall apart.

* * * *

Max walked into the kitchen and stopped when he so Bo sitting with his head in his hands and his bottom lip quivering. Fear shot through Max and had him thundering across the small space to reach Bo. He'd known something was off when Bo hadn't been on the porch to greet him like he usually did, but he'd almost convinced himself he was being paranoid and that Bo was just in the bathroom or something.

Well, he'd damn sure listen to his instincts next time, if there was a next time. *There'd better not be a next time.* He was beside Bo in two heartbeats, and his lover stood and plastered himself to Max, his arms locking around him tightly as Max held Bo in return.

"What happened, honey?" He could feel Bo shuddering, hear his breath hitching as he swallowed noisily. "Bo? Honey can you tell me what's wrong?"

Bo made an agonised sound that twisted Max's guts into a fiery knot. "Detective Sanchez called and said…" Max brought a hand up to cup the back of Bo's head. He rubbed gently, letting the silky strands slide between his fingers as he tried not to push Bo.

"They arrested him," Bo finally whispered, then repeated it when Max only grunted. The truth was, he couldn't speak just yet, he was too angry and relieved and so many other things he couldn't keep track. Instead Max kept caressing Bo, and trailing soft kisses over his brow. Bo shuddered again then sighed shakily before tipping his head up to look at Max.

Max stared into those hazel eyes he knew so well, looking for pain or guilt. He saw a little of both, but he mainly saw relief.

"He tried to hurt another man, but he fucked up and picked a guy who taught martial arts of some kind. The guy beat the hell out of the man who assaulted me — Louis

Christopher is his name." Bo's grin was a bit watery as he continued. "I'll need to testify, and so will the man who put the smackdown to Christopher, plus there might be other victims who come forward, but—"

This time when Bo smiled, it did that thing Max loved, the one that lit the man up from the inside out. "They got him. They got him, Max, and I don't care what his lawyers try to say about me, I'm going to make sure that asshole goes to jail as long as possible."

"He will." Max was worried about what Bo would have to go through on the stand, but there was always the chance Christopher would plead guilty and get a lighter sentence. The idea of that made Max's blood boil, but if it saved Bo from going through something that might be almost as bad as the assault, then Max was all for it. And he firmly believed Christopher would get what he had coming, either in prison or elsewhere. To think anything else was unbearable.

But, if the case did go to trial, then Max would be right there in the court room, as close to Bo as he could get. He'd support his partner all the way, and try not to lose it and do anything stupid like attempt to rip off that asshole's head. Chance and Rory would probably be there too, and likely some other people Max and Bo had got to know and become friends with. It might not just be Max who had to try to keep from going after Christopher, come to think of it.

"We should celebrate."

Bo's whispered words snapped Max out of his daze. He smiled and lowered a hand to Bo's ass. He'd have asked if Bo was sure, but the man was rubbing his groin against Max's thigh eagerly, and soft pants were slipping from his lips. Max's concern for what would happen should there be a trial or if Christopher pled out didn't vanish, but he did push it down.

Bo wanted to celebrate, and that was something Max was happy to do with his man.

Chapter Eighteen

If Bo had thought he was nervous the day before, it was nothing compared to when he woke up on Valentine's Day. Max had made love to him almost all night long, making sure Bo knew just how precious he was to Max, how loved he was. Those doubts that used to plague Bo still cropped up sometimes, but usually all he had to do was close his eyes and think about the way Max touched him, kissed him, and so many little things the man did for him. Of course Max did big things too, but Bo had found it was the sweet little moments in day to day life with each other that really melted his heart.

However, he suspected today would be one of the 'big thing' days, and was worried his rather boring gifts to Max would not be adequate to show his love. Oh, Max would be happy with anything, and he'd never say a cruel word about Bo's gifts, but...Bo wanted to make Max as happy, make him feel as loved as Max made him feel.

And I thought I could do that by getting him the same damn gifts desperate, unimaginative men everywhere give their women? Idiot! Shit, now was a fine time to come to that realisation. He couldn't slip off without making it obvious he hadn't got Max something, even though he had. It just wasn't anything special. *Damn it!*

Bo eased out of the bed, careful not to wake Max. As he quietly left the room, a plan niggled at Bo's brain. It wasn't the best one in the world, but it was his only one, and it wasn't a horrible idea either. Feeling somewhat more secure about his gifts, Bo set about getting started.

* * * *

Max groaned and stretched as he woke up, one hand automatically patting the bed as he felt around for Bo. When his fingers encountered cool sheets where his lover usually lay, Max cracked open his eyes and propped himself up on one elbow. He blinked away the blurries and stared stupidly at the empty spot on the bed. Obviously Bo wasn't there. *Duh, nitwit. I need some coffee.* Max flopped back on the bed and slapped an arm over his eyes. Then the scent hit him. And his mental calendar squawked.

Valentine's Day. *Shit. Shit! What if Bo hates what I got him?* Max would likely die from humiliation. It wasn't that Bo would laugh at him, or be a jerk about it, but he just might not want what Max was going to give him. The thought of that made Max's stomach burn. The smell of something delicious wafting through the partially opened bedroom door made his stomach growl.

Despite being so nervous his hands shook, Max got up and found a pair of underwear to put on. Just because he and Bo were the only ones in the bunkhouse now didn't mean they'd be the only ones here period. Max added a pair of sweats with that thought bouncing around his head, then he padded to the bathroom and took care of business before heading to the kitchen.

Max sucked in a sharp breath when he stepped into the room. Bo jumped but grinned at him over a bare shoulder. Max tried to reciprocate but damn, all his muscles seemed to have locked in place and his cock was trying to poke a hole through his shorts and sweats as he gawped at Bo.

Bo's grin widened and he winked at Max. "I thought I'd try to start your Valentine's off right since I think I bumbled the whole gift thing." Bo shook his completely bare ass, framed by the strings of a bright yellow apron, as he gestured with one hand to the table.

"If this is the only gift I get, I'm the luckiest damn man in the world," Max muttered as he dragged his gaze up to Bo's happy face and back down to his tempting plump ass. Max's mouth watered as he ogled those firm, fuzzy globes. He'd been thinking about, wanting to try…

Not yet, Jesus not yet! As much as Max wanted to spread those cheeks and explore every bit of warm skin there, he couldn't. Well, he *could*, but he really wanted to wait until he'd given Bo his other gift first. Max settled for pressing his front to Bo's back and grinding his aching cock against that delectable ass as he nibbled on Bo's neck.

Bo moaned softly, then a little louder when Max suckled the sweet spot where Bo's shoulder and neck met. "B-bacon," Bo stuttered out. "Burning—"

Max debated letting it burn for a second before remembering all Bo had protecting his bits was a thin apron. He left off sucking on Bo's neck but slid his hands under the apron and cupped Bo's balls and cock as best he could. "Maxie!" Bo squeaked. "Not helping!"

"Just trying to keep you from getting hurt," Max said in what he hoped was a sexy purr. Bo had that purring thing down pat, and it never failed to set Max's heart—and other parts — to fluttering. Judging by the way Bo shivered, he must have pulled the purring thing off pretty well, too.

"Bacon's done, if you'll just have a seat." Bo sounded a little breathless, and Max was wearing a smug grin when he released him and turned to walk to the table. Max stumbled when he saw his place setting and the flowers and heart-shaped box of chocolates there. The card laid on his plate had his name written — well, Maxie, his pet name from Bo — in fancy script. The envelope was decorated with one single, hand drawn heart on the upper left corner, and for some reason that sent a wave of warmth through Max.

"Is it okay?" Bo asked from behind him. Max heard the worry in his lover's voice and turned, intending to take Bo in his arms and make love to him right then and there, never mind the plans he had for later. He was thwarted by the platter of bacon Bo held in one hand and the stacked platter of waffles he had in the other.

"It's more than okay," Max said after swallowing around a lump of emotion in his throat. "Nobody ever gave me flowers and hearts before. The only cards I ever got were this past Christmas from Rory and Chance and the rest of our friends. Thank you, Bo." Max leaned in carefully and kissed Bo's soft lips. When he leant back Bo's eyes were shining happily and his smile was that bright one that Max loved to see.

"I know they aren't the most original gifts, but since you never got them before, I'm really glad to be the first person to give them to you."

Max didn't know how it was possible considering everything in his world revolved around the man already, but he fell even more in love with Bo right then and there. He took the platters from Bo and gave him another kiss, this one longer, a little messy, but it made them both hum with happiness before he turned and walked to the table.

After setting the food down, he took his seat and carefully opened the card. The message was brief, but it hit Max square in the heart. His eyes blurred as he closed the card and tucked it back in the envelope. Then he started to push his chair back but Bo was right there, draping himself over Max's back and craning his neck to bring his lips to Max's.

By the time the kiss ended, Max's cock was so hard he couldn't sit comfortably. Taking Bo back to bed seemed like the best idea ever, then he noticed the meal Bo had prepared. Homemade waffles, fresh strawberries and some blueberry compote that Max nearly drooled over, ice cream in a beautiful ceramic bowl Max hadn't a clue they'd had, and what he thought was whipped cream. Max arched a brow and pointed towards the thick white stuff.

"Is that whipped cream?"

Bo nodded. "Homemade, too. It doesn't take long and it tastes so much better than the store bought stuff." He beamed at Max and pushed the bowl towards him. "I suggest waffles, ice cream, whipped cream, then the blueberries and strawberries. And bacon on the side, of course. Can't have you missing out on your meat." Bo leered and winked at that last bit.

Max chuckled and stacked the food according to Bo's suggestion. The first bite made Max moan as his eyes closed. He hadn't had anything this good in...ever.

"I used to make this every now and then years ago, when I wanted something decadent for breakfast."

Max opened his eyes and Bo blushed as he glanced down at the feast. "I never made it for anyone else," he said softly, and Max thought he was possibly glowing like Bo did, just lighting up from the inside out.

"Thank you, honey. You don't know how much all of this means to me." Max wasn't sure he could tell Bo, either, but he hoped to show him later.

They took their time eating breakfast, enjoying one another's company and sharing heated glances. The buildup of anticipation was almost as delicious as the meal, and Max savoured every second of it. Afterwards he insisted on Bo relaxing while he cleaned up the table and the dishes, then Max had to go check the horses.

Bo came along to help, and together they got the horses fed and watered and their stalls clean. Then Max told Bo to hop in the shower, and all the nerves Max had managed came roaring back as he saddled two horses before heading to the bunkhouse to clean up.

* * * *

He'd thought breakfast went well enough. Bo replayed the morning in his head. Yeah, Max had been glowing with joy, so where had it gone wrong? Why was he in here showering by himself when he'd been so sure Max wouldn't be able to wait to get his hands on him?

Bo didn't know whether to be worried or not. Max hadn't seemed upset, although he'd started to look a bit nervous once they finished taking care of the horses. And Max hadn't given him anything for Valentine's Day yet, which Bo wasn't exactly worried about. He wasn't with Max to see what he could get from the man, but he was a little surprised Max hadn't done *something* yet.

Unless…Bo remembered the whole 'big thing' idea. Some of the tension drained out of him. That fit. Max probably had something planned, and it was going to bowl Bo right over, just like he had when he'd given Bo that beautiful roan mare, or when he'd sung Bo a love song in a surprisingly lovely baritone. Or like the time he'd spent hours massaging and kissing every inch of Bo's body. Those might not have been 'big things' to anyone else, but to Bo they were colossal, and he had trouble believing he deserved them.

But to doubt he did implied Max was wrong in believing in him, and so Bo tried to silence that doubtful, nagging voice with the sound of Max's soothing, reassuring one.

And now, he was pretty sure there was another 'big thing' coming, and even though he didn't know what it was, he thought it'd be the biggest yet.

Bo got out of the shower and towelled off quickly, both nervous and eager to see what Max had planned. He rushed from the bathroom into the bedroom and pulled up short to leer at Max as the man bent to pull off his sweats and underwear. "Mmm, baby, you sure have a fine ass," Bo purred, unable to stay silent when he looked at that firm flesh. His dick sprang to full mast and he palmed it loosely as Max blushed from thighs to cheeks when he turned to Bo. "Any chance you want to mess around a little before you shower?"

Max arched a brow and looked at Bo's hand on his cock. "A little? I'm thinking it'd take more than a little to satisfy that hard on you got."

"Well yeah," Bo acknowledged easily. "But what other plans have we got?"

Max's cheeks darkened and he grinned that easy, laid back grin that had first drawn Bo in. "You'll have to wait and see. Why don't you get dressed and all moisturised and stuff while I shower?"

Bo was disappointed and so curious he almost bounced with anticipation upon hearing his theory confirmed. He didn't even argue, although he did grab Max for a dirty grind and a hungry kiss when the man tried to walk past. Bo also added a good slap to one firm cheek that made Max yelp then shake his butt before disappearing into the bathroom. Then he set about getting ready as he hummed the love song Max had sung to him.

Chapter Nineteen

Max was glad Bo had been so excited when he'd seen the horses saddled up and ready to go. This was the most romantic thing Max could think of, and he knew by the sappy smile on Bo's face and the tender glances from the man that Bo thought it was pretty romantic, too, especially once he realised where they were headed. Bo didn't say anything, but Max would swear he could see every bit of the joy Bo felt in those pretty hazel eyes.

They rode together in companionable silence, except for a few words here and there, or when Bo hummed a tune Max had sung to him one night months ago. Max had joined in, humming along for a line or two before singing instead. And damned if Bo didn't just glow.

Once they reached the spot by the stream where they'd first made love, Max dismounted and helped Bo do the same. Not that Bo wasn't perfectly capable, but they both enjoyed it when Max helped. There was lots of touching and that long glide of Bo's body sliding against his once he finally got out of the saddle.

And kisses, Max wouldn't trade those kisses for anything. Long and slow, hard and deep, saying so much more than words could sometimes. By the time they stepped apart, they were both breathing heavily and a bit glassy-eyed. Well, Bo was, and Max figured he had to look about the same.

"Got to tie the horses," he rasped. Bo nodded and Max took the reins from his hands. "Can you get the blanket and pouch from my saddle bags?"

"Yeah," Bo murmured, his voice as rough as Max's. "Do you—can we put the blanket in the same spot?"

Max nodded as he waited for Bo to retrieve the items. "Yeah, that's what I had in mind." He watched closely as Bo pulled a small, prettily wrapped gift from the saddle bag. The way Bo frowned was kind of worrisome, but maybe it was just because Bo didn't know what was in the box. It was long and rectangular, and Max knew Bo would likely have some idea that was close to the truth soon enough. Turning, he sighed and hoped he wasn't fixing to screw everything up. He led the horses to a thick branch and tied them there then walked to where Bo was now spreading the blanket out.

Max helped settle the corners and smooth out the worst of the wrinkles before taking one of Bo's hands in his. He looked at the gift setting on the ground right beside the blanket then back at Bo, who was frowning again.

"You're starting to worry me," Max told him when Bo's frown deepened. Bo blinked and looked at him. His lips tipped up slightly and he gestured at the present. "I'm just trying to see through that pretty gold paper. Trying to decide if there's jewellery," Bo's eyebrows arched as his voice hitched higher into a questioning tone. "Or...or what? I don't know. I'm leaning towards jewellery. A watch, bracelet, or maybe a necklace? It's driving me nuts not knowing."

Now or never. "Well, we can't have that," Max said, glad his voice didn't quaver. "Wait right here." He squeezed Bo's hand then went and picked up the box. Turning back around was hard, because his knees seemed to have turned into jelly or something, but Max locked gazes with Bo and found the strength to hold it together and go through with his plan. He just hoped to hell Bo didn't freak out.

When Max was a couple of feet away, he slowed even more. Bo's eyes never left his, and when Max dropped to one knee in front of Bo, those eyes nearly bugged right out of his head. Max's heart pounded so hard in his chest his ribs hurt, but his voice was steady as he pulled the ribbon off the gift and popped the box open.

* * * *

Bo had stopped breathing when Max had knelt in front of him, but seeing the glistening rings in the box had him sucking in so much air his lungs burned. Max had tricked him but good, having the jewellery put in a rectangular box. Bo would have recognised a ring box, even if he'd never been given one before. He'd seen enough of them on TV and such. Then it hit Bo, really hit him what it meant to have Max down on one knee, holding a box with two men's wedding rings in them, and he got dizzy as adrenalin flooded his system. Joy and a bit of fear chased after it, but before Bo could do more than kind of squeak, Max took his left hand.

"I'm not the best with words, but I'm just going to say what I feel and hope that's okay."

Bo nodded, not trusting himself to make another embarrassing sound. He held Max's hand tightly, trying to blink away tear-blurred vision. He didn't want to miss seeing a second of this.

Max took a deep breath then blew it out. "Bo Jenkins, I've loved you almost since the day we met. No one ever moved me like you did, and still do. I figured I'd spend my life alone, then one day you came into my world and shook it up in the best way possible. Now, I know it ain't legal for two men to get married in this state, but I don't care. We can go somewhere it is legal, and we can have a small ceremony here at the ranch or wherever you want, too." Max's Adam's apple bobbed twice then his eyes glistened with moisture. "Bo, will you marry me? I'll be the best man I can be, and make sure you're always taken care of, always loved, if you'll have me."

"Yes," Bo said without having to think about it. "Yes, oh God, yes!" He dropped to his knees and set the box down beside him so he could cup Max's cheek. Then he kissed his man, infusing every bit of the love filling him, healing wounds that had yet to mend with each sweet stroke of lips and tongue.

Max lifted his lips from Bo's and looked down. He took the rings from the box and held out his hand. Bo's trembled as he placed his in Max's. "It's okay if I put it on you now?" Max asked. Bo nodded, eager to feel that band around his finger. Max slid the ring over the tip of Bo's ring finger then watched him while he slowly pushed the ring into place. "I love you more than I can ever tell you," Max murmured.

Bo gave up trying not to cry and let the tears spill down his cheeks. He took the other ring from Max and held out his hand. As he slid the band into place, he vowed to love Max for the rest of their lives, and if possible, thereafter too. He sealed his vow with another kiss then slowly began undressing his fiancé.

"Fiancé," Bo murmured between kisses to Max's neck. "I like saying that."

"Mmm," Max hummed, "I think I'll like 'husband' even better. You just say when and where and we'll do it."

"I'll think on that later. Right now I want you in me," Bo said as he worked the shirt off Max's shoulders. They took their time getting undressed, touching and kissing each other as more skin was bared. Once they were naked, Max gently eased Bo down onto the blanket before picking up his jeans and pulling out a packet of lube. They'd agreed to stop using condoms since they were solid, completely committed to each other.

"I'm going to make love to you for hours," Max promised as he settled on his side by Bo. Any answer Bo might have made was swallowed by Max as he kissed Bo breathless.

Max nipped at that spot that made Bo boneless. His back arched as Max nibbled his way down to Bo's nipple. Max worked the sensitive bud with his teeth first while he used one hand to give attention to the other nipple.

"Please, Max, Maxie," Bo panted as sharp spikes of pleasure spread from his chest. Max rumbled something Bo didn't understand, but it didn't matter because Max finally began sliding down his body, stopping occasionally to suck up a mark on Bo's skin.

Bo squirmed and moaned; he fisted his hands in Max's hair and tried to push him down closer to his dick. Max's chuckle sent goose bumps over Bo's skin. "Please, pleasepleaseplease," Bo gibbered, mindless from the pleasure zinging through his body.

"Soon, honey."

Bo sobbed with relief when Max's head dipped lower, then he whined when Max licked the juncture of groin and thigh, bypassing Bo's aching dick. Max's hands slid under Bo to cup his ass, and that felt good, but Bo needed more.

Then Max pushed, tipping Bo's hips up, and something wet and firm slicked over Bo's hole. He shouted in surprise as nerve endings in that hidden place shot to life. "M-Max," Bo gasped, his lungs pumping like bellows. Max had never done that before, had never even said anything—"Unngh!" Bo grunted as he tried to shove his butt down or up or wherever he could to get that tongue teasing around his opening to actually penetrate him. A puff of warm air wafted over his wet skin, then thumbs pried his cheeks apart and Max began eating his ass like he'd been doing it for years.

Bo whimpered when that slick muscle shoved into his ass, then keened when Max sealed his lips around Bo's pucker and sucked. He wailed when a thumb slipped in with Max's tongue, and Bo couldn't do anything but writhe and make sounds he'd never heard pass his lips before. His cock throbbed and his balls drew tight as Max rimmed him until Bo begged with his body and slurred words for more.

Only then did Max lift his head and kiss the inside of each of Bo's thighs. "I guess I did that right," Max said and Bo just nodded as he trembled with need.

Bo watched as Max pushed himself up until he was kneeling between Bo's legs, then he grabbed the packet of lube and opened it. Once his cock was glistening with the thick liquid, Max hooked his arms around Bo's thighs and hitched his butt right up onto Max's lap. Bo tried to help, but he seemed to have lost all muscle control thanks to Max's talented mouth. He felt the prod of Max's dick at his hole and struggled to keep his eyes open. He might not be able to do much yet, but he sure as hell wanted to see Max's face as he slid that cock into his ass.

Then Bo found he could do something as Max began pressing that thick length into him. Bo opened his mouth and let out the words that filled him near to bursting with happiness. "I love you, Maxie."

Max shuddered and filled Bo's ass with one long thrust. "God, honey, I love you too, but I can't...think. Your ass is so tight and hot..." Max broke off with a moan as he began rocking his hips, burrowing his cock in so deep Bo could feel each push rippling up to his belly. "God!"

Bo dragged his arms up, holding them open. Max grunted and dropped down on top of him, pressing Bo down into the ground. Bo locked his legs around Max's waist and arched his back, mewling as Max's cock brushed over his gland.

The sound seemed to set Max off. He growled and kissed Bo fiercely before pushing up on his elbows and pounding his dick into Bo's ass. Bo's body lit up like a fireworks display on the Fourth of July. He gasped then shouted as Max's balls slapped his, the bite of pain amplifying the ecstasy swirling in Bo. Max's stomach ground against Bo's cock, providing the friction he needed to send him over the edge.

Bo jerked and whimpered, panting as his cock painted his stomach and chest with cum. His inner muscles clamped tight and Max hollered, tossing his head back so the corded muscles and tendons in his neck stood out as his dick throbbed inside Bo. Hot spunk filled Bo's ass as Max pounded into him one more time then stilled as he shoved his groin against Bo's butt. His hips jutted in rapid, erratic bursts as he came, whispering Bo's name over and over.

Max lowered himself down slowly until he was lying on Bo once again. Bo didn't mind the weight at all. He loved feeling Max's body on his any way he could get it. He slid his hands up Max's sweat slicked skin, pausing only once he reached the tops of Max's shoulders. There the sunlight on his wedding ring caught his eye, and Bo held Max tightly.

"As soon as we can, wherever we can," Bo whispered, knowing Max would understand.

Max kissed him softly on the cheek, then more firmly on the lips. His darks eyes glowed with happiness when he lifted his mouth enough to say, "Anything you want, honey."

Bo smiled back. When it came down to it, he already had everything he wanted, although being married would be awesome. But as long as he had Max, he'd be happy, and he intended to spend the rest of his life making sure Max was just as happy, too.

About the Author

A native Texan, Bailey spends her days spinning stories around in her head, which has contributed to more than one incident of tripping over her own feet. Evenings are reserved for pounding away at the keyboard, as are early morning hours. Sleep? Doesn't happen much. Writing is too much fun, and there are too many characters bouncing about, tapping on Bailey's brain demanding to be let out.

Caffeine and chocolate are permanent fixtures in Bailey's office and are never far from hand at any given time. Removing either of those necessities from Bailey's presence can result in what is known as A Very, Very Scary Bailey and is not advised under any circumstances.

Bailey Bradford loves to hear from readers. You can find her contact information, website details and author profile page at http://www.total-e-bound.com.

Total-E-Bound Publishing

www.total-e-bound.com

Take a look at our exciting range of literagasmic™
erotic romance titles and discover pure quality
at Total-E-Bound.